THE LAST FEW MILES OF ROAD

THE LAST FEW MILES OF ROAD

A CARTER McCOY NOVEL

ERIC BEETNER

LEVEL
BEST BOOKS

First published by Level Best Books 2024

This novel is entirely a work of fiction. The names, characters and incidents portrayed in it are the work of the author's imagination. Any resemblance to actual persons, living or dead, events or localities is entirely coincidental.

Eric Beetner asserts the moral right to be identified as the author of this work.

Author Photo Credit: Mark Krajnak

First edition

ISBN: 978-1-68512-577-6

Cover art by Level Best Designs

This book was professionally typeset on Reedsy.
Find out more at reedsy.com

To Marie – who faced the darkness and stood strong

Praise for The Last Few Miles of Road

"Featuring an anti-hero straight out of an Elmore Leonard novel, *The Last Few Miles of Road* is a twisty-turny country noir with a heart of gold. Beetner conjures up a cast of memorably heartbreaking characters, featuring an angel of death killer trying to make the world better, one hit at a time, and a femme fatale in the guise of a desperate teenager, eager to live a better life than the one she was dealt. Carter and Bree are the 21st century Bonnie and Clyde, and I can't wait to see what's next for them!"—Halley Sutton, *USA Today* bestselling author of *The Hurricane Blonde*

"Beetner breaks out with *The Last Few Miles of Road,* a perfectly crafted crime story. Terminally-ill vigilante Carter McCoy is the hero we've been waiting for, finding purpose and connection in his waning days as he weighs the moral burden of taking justice into his own hands. I absolutely loved it."—Laura McHugh, award-winning author of *What's Done in Darkness*

"Beetner has spun another notable tale here. Noir at its best."—David Swinson, author of *The Second Girl* and *Sweet Thing*

ONE

Carter McCoy closed the menu and handed it back to the waitress. "Y'know what? Screw it, I'll have the butter burger. Grilled onions. And fries." He smiled at her, and it made the wrinkles in his cheeks deeper. She smiled back, the way a kid looks at their grandparent. "And a chocolate shake," he added. "Only live once, right?"

She wrote it down and went away with a grin. He had all the hallmarks of a kind old man. Snow white hair, still mostly there. Wrinkles around the corners of his mouth and his eyes. Laugh lines, they called them. Seventy-two years old but could pass for sixty-two if he wanted. Still spry, still active, still life in his light brown eyes.

"Not for long," Carter said quietly.

And it wasn't because of the butter burger, a regional specialty, and nemesis to cardiologists everywhere. He chose the diner not because he liked it or because they served the greaseball Midwestern staple, but for proximity. The diner sat half a block from the hospital he'd just come from. It was still inside a half an hour from when the doctor told him the name of the disease that would kill him. All nine syllables of it. Carter refused to remember what it was. He didn't want the name of his assassin on his lips. What did it matter anyhow?

He got the standard response. Six months, maybe more, maybe less. What they said when they had no clue when he'd go. "Maybe less" could mean he'd hit the deck before he reached the elevator.

The bottom line was, nothing they could do. Carter had contracted an extremely rare disorder, the doctor had told him with some degree of respect for the elusive disease, that's why it had taken so long to diagnose properly.

All those months spent wondering, speculating, testing when Carter could have done something more with his days if he'd known they were among his last.

Now he knew what he had to do, though. Eat the cheeseburgers and milkshakes he hadn't been able to in years. Never mind what they did to his stomach. Drink the good scotch. Watch the sunsets and sleep through the sunrises.

And finish a bit of business he'd left undone for far too long. A task he should have taken care of years ago. A balancing of the scales.

He needed to kill a man.

The idea had been there in the back of his brain for decades now. Like how he kept saying he was going to pick up his guitar again. His wife kept him from the thoughts of killing this man most of the time, but Ava was gone six years now. By then, it had gone so long undone that the deed no longer seemed like it needed doing. But with his diagnosis, Carter knew this would be his final act. He could not go off into the long dark forever without doing this one thing.

For her.

He and Ava had one child, a daughter named Audrey. She died twenty-one years before. And Carter was going to kill the man who did it.

The urge began right after it happened. What father wouldn't want to kill the one who took his daughter from him? But he let the system work. He went to the trial every day. Watched as they gave him a charge of negligent homicide and, with his prior convictions on a number of charges, sentenced him to twelve years in prison.

Justin Lyons was his name. He served eight years and then got out to live the rest of his life while Audrey laid cold in the ground under six feet of earth.

Carter had kept up with him, his address, his run-ins with the law. He kept it from Ava, but he knew the man lived less than twenty miles away. He knew the man worked only menial jobs, incurred one drunk and disorderly charge ten years ago. Justin Lyons lived a small, unremarkable life, but better than no life at all.

His cheeseburger came. He could only eat half, and he left half the milkshake in the glass. He tipped the smiling girl twenty dollars on a twelve-dollar check and left the diner knowing two things: he was dying soon, and so was Justin Lyons.

His truck kicked up dirt behind him, even on the paved roads. It had been a dry year so far, and the fields on either side of the two-lane, which usually stood knee-high with corn, lay empty with their ridges of soil like a giant fork had been dragged through the earth. Dust blew freely; the flat upper-Midwestern plains offered little resistance to any wind that happened along.

Carter was out of town quickly and on the road toward where his house stood perched in what the politicians called "the heartland" and what people who lived there called "That big empty nowhere."

He never planned to live in a farmhouse. Just worked out that way. Carter turned off the road and onto his long dirt path toward the house. Shallow ditches ran along either side, and in a good spring, they'd fill with frogs chirping, but now all they grew were weeds. More clouds rose up behind him before falling back down like a would-be dust storm, giving up in defeat. The dirt filled in the tracks of his tires, hiding any evidence that he was ever there.

He parked the truck by the side of the house and sat behind the wheel for a good long while, feeling the burger in his gut and also hearing the doctor's words reverberate in his head. By the time he snapped out of it, he had no idea how long he'd been sitting there. He shut off the truck, got out, and didn't lock it, then walked up the creaky steps to the door.

Carter sat in the good chair in his living room with the lights off and watched as the sun set outside the windows and the room grew slowly darker.

"I wonder if this will be what it's like," he said aloud. "Nah, probably not. It'll go quicker. I hope."

Since Ava died, he'd taken to talking to himself. With no one around to hear him, he knew it didn't sound crazy to anyone but himself, and the sound of his own voice kept him company.

His big lunch still sat in his stomach like a pound of lead, so he reclined there a little longer, not worried about dinner. He was surprised to find himself not worried about anything anymore. He thought the diagnosis would be a huge weight pressing down on him, but instead, he felt a lightness now. He could see the finish line after a long journey.

There was a certain freedom in knowing when the ending will arrive, even if he didn't know the exact date. And he'd done enough with his life to not feel any pressure to cram it all in before the curtain fell.

He built a good small business running movie theaters. He'd gone from one screen in town to six spread out over the whole county until he got bought out twenty years ago by one of the big chains. It left him with enough money to retire on and live comfortably. Add on Ava's life insurance, and he was doing fine in his small and inexpensive life, even if he lived another thirty years.

A heart attack took her. It snuck up and brought her down by surprise, like a cat sneaking up on a beautiful bird. Drawn by instinct and the bird's beautiful plumage, it leapt, cutting her song short. Not like Carter. Ava didn't have to deal with this waiting around for the killer you know is in the house to leap out from the shadows.

She was the only woman he ever knew who died of a heart attack. You think of it more for men with fists of raw meat in their chests, which finally give out when they catch the men doing things they shouldn't.

He missed her every day, same as he missed Audrey. That eased the pain of the diagnosis, too. If Ava was still around, he would fight the inevitable and rage against it to stay even one more day by her side. But without her and nearly a lifetime without his daughter, he felt it easier to loosen his grip on the rope and let go.

After he'd taken care of his unfinished business.

The windows were open all around the first floor of the house, trying to coax in a slight breeze. The air had turned hot in the past week, and it would stay there through the summer. Carter hoped he got to make it to one more fall, his favorite season. He was not a man built for humidity. Carter stood and turned on a floor lamp. It threw the room into shadows and light. He stepped to the photo of Ava on the mantle.

"I wish I was the kind of guy who could say 'see you soon', but we both know that wasn't us." He could hear her laugh still like it was a scent lingering in the carpets. "I'm gonna do a thing," he said and averted his eyes from the picture. "A thing you wouldn't approve of. I guess I'm sorry about that, but it's my choice to make now."

He went to the fridge, deciding he could eat again. The shelves were nearly bare. In that moment, he decided he wasn't going to go through the hassle of cooking for the rest of his life. The phrase made Carter smile. He could declare a lot of things done *for the rest of his life*. Shaving, for one. Cutting his hair. Brushing his teeth. He second thought that one. Even if no one else had to smell his breath, he still had to live with himself for a few months. Hopefully, it would be months.

He took the keys off the hook and didn't have to think about where he would go to eat. At least twice a week since Ava died, and at least once a week when she was alive, Carter ate at Mesa Grande. A little family-run place that made the best enchiladas with green sauce he'd ever had. Killer guacamole and a homemade horchata that he drank by the gallon. Minnesota wasn't exactly the epicenter for Mexican cuisine, but he'd never had better.

He reached the door and heard a familiar sound. The owner, a guy named Eddie, was swearing a blue streak at his wife, Ivana. He did it when the place was empty, and he thought no one could hear, but did it loud enough so anyone passing by or pulling into the parking lot could hear clearly. Ivana was from Central America, did the cooking and really ran the place. Eddie opened the joint for her, but really he just did it to make a buck off his wife's culinary gifts. Carter had always felt like Ivana was a bit trapped with him, probably took his marriage proposal as a quick and easy way to stay in the States. He didn't know the real backstory, but he always looked when Ivana came to the table to take an order to see whether she had a shiner or not.

He and Ava were long-time regulars at Mesa Grande. Ivana would come out of the back with that beaten-dog look and break into a smile when she saw them.

"The usual?" she'd ask. Carter always nodded and said yes. Ava always played at scouring the menu, but nine times out of ten settled on the same tostada salad with pork.

Carter hovered outside the door a minute, listening. Eddie had gone out back to smoke one of his cigars and was yelling at her through the screen door. The air hung stagnant around him, and Carter could hear moths slap against the overhead light in the breaks when Eddie would suck on his cigar and think of a new insult for his wife.

"I swear to God," Eddie said. "You're so goddamn lucky to have me. Think about where you'd be if it wasn't for me. No education. All you can do is cook. You think you'd be more grateful."

Carter knew Ivana was a Catholic, and he'd seen her flinch each time someone took the lord's name in vain. Even if he didn't believe, he'd tried to curb the goddamns in her restaurant. Like a decent human being. But her religion and her upbringing meant divorce was a sin. And even if she did leave him, what options did she have? He'd take the restaurant from her, probably their daughter too, out of spite. Ivana was trapped.

"Lucky you're good in the sack," Eddie said. "And hey, speaking of—"

"Eddie!" Ivana's only pushback was ever the one word. It meant everything from "Knock it off" to "Please be quiet" to "Shut your fucking mouth we got customers."

Carter felt a strange pull in his chest. For a second, he worried it was a heart attack until he recognized it as a different kind of clench. His whole body tensed like a fist gripped in anger. And then he felt what wasn't there—fear. Worry of consequences. He was dying soon; what was there to worry about?

Carter pushed open the door, and a tiny bell rang over his head. He saw Ivana's smile break across her face. He didn't stop in his regular booth and walked right past the counter, his own face set in stone.

10

"Carter, how have you been?" she asked.

He nodded once to her. "Ivana." He went behind the counter and through the kitchen. Ivana was confused and, after hesitating, followed him.

Carter slapped open the screen door and walked into a cloud of stink from the combo of the cigar and trash pile. In the midst of it, like a foul odor himself, Eddie turned. He wasn't expecting anyone but his wife. Eddie rarely made conversation with the customers, and Carter couldn't tell if he recognized him at all despite the years of lining Eddie's pockets from weekly meals. His face was all shock and worry. Carter wondered what he might have to worry about, but dismissed the thought.

Without thinking too hard about it, he stepped close to Eddie, swung his hand out, palm flat, and slapped the cigar out of his mouth, catching a good deal of cheek as he went. The sound was almost louder than the screen door clapping shut behind him.

Carter balled his hand into a fist with his index finger pointed sharply out and aiming at Eddie's face like it was a nail he was lining up to drive home.

"I ever hear you talk to her like that again, and I'll come back here and slap more than the cigar out of your mouth. I'll slap your teeth out. You hear me?"

Eddie didn't need to know it had been more than fifty years since Carter had been in a fight. Not since his time in the army had he caused even the slightest physical damage to another person. His eyes said differently, though.

"Who the hell are—"

Carter slapped him again. "You're done talking tonight. Why don't you take care of this trash out here? It stinks. But maybe that's just you."

He wished he had planned some things to say, maybe sound a little more believably threatening. He kept up the hard face, though, a red flush rising on his cheeks. Part was the anger, and part was knowing he should have done this years ago.

Behind him, Ivana held herself in the doorway with her arms folded tight against her chest, both silent and still.

Carter got his finger right up close to Eddie's eye. "Just watch your fuckin' mouth."

He turned and walked back through the kitchen. Ivana stayed hugging herself as she moved aside to let him pass.

"The usual, please," he said as he went to take a seat at the counter.

Eddie watched him go, slack-jawed. The screen door swung back into place with a smack. Eddie outside, alone. Ivana turned and went into the kitchen to start cooking. Eddie remained still for a while, then took two bags of garbage and walked them over to the dumpster.

A minute later, Carter heard Eddie's car pull out of the lot. When Ivana set his plate down, she said nothing but paused, putting her hand on his wrist. Her palm was still warm from the hot plate, and he felt that warmth move through his body in a way he hadn't experienced in years. Another human's touch. It didn't matter that it was a woman; there was nothing romantic about it. But it made Carter realize he couldn't name the last time he had touched another person.

She turned up the music a little louder to fill the space, and he ate in silence. A couple came in, and she busied herself with their order, stopping to refill his horchata on one pass by the counter. He waited until she disappeared into the back before he left without saying goodbye or discussing what had happened, but he left twice the amount on the check.

Carter felt twenty years younger. Standing up to a bully, acting like a tough guy. Damn, it was a high. But back in his house, belly full and his eyes tired, the come-down came fast.

"Too bad you're dying," he said.

His bravery felt suddenly false. The only reason he'd done it was that he had nothing to lose. He never fully understood that saying. But now he had no life to lose, no people. But there was always something. He did have people. Their memories. Was anyone still around to remember Ava? Her parents and brother were gone. Her friends, mostly.

And Audrey. Gone when she was twenty-one. Did anyone in the bloom of youth back then still remember the girl who died tragically? Was she just a story without a face or a name? When he went, her memory might fade into darkness like a campfire, leaving only smoke to waft away on a breeze.

He *did* have things to lose, still. Including time.

Carter sat in the living room, listening to how quiet the house had become. Ava liked to play music all the time. Low murmuring sounds in the background, melodies that reminded her of youth and people she once knew. Carter spent most of his time in silence for the same reasons: because the songs made him think of people and of the past.

He tried watching game shows or lawyer dramas, but he felt like an old man. They park them in front of TVs at nursing homes while Wheel Of Fortune drones on, and he never wanted to feel that way. So he did puzzles, read books, did crosswords. Mind stimulation, fending off dementia and memory loss, even though there were many times he wished he could forget

13

certain things selectively, like weeding a garden.

It came over him that he didn't want to live out the rest of his life in silence.

He stood and went to the second floor. He turned on the hall light and stopped halfway, reached up, and pulled on the short rope to the attic hatch. It folded down with a great groan of the springs. He couldn't remember the last time he'd been to the attic. Not since he'd moved some of Ava's things up there. He unfolded the ladder and pressed on it to make sure it was secure and locked in place. He started his slow climb.

Some brave man, slapping cigars out of bullies mouths. Afraid of tumbling off a ladder and breaking a hip.

He reached the top and felt around in the darkness for the pull string to the light. He was surprised when the single bulb came on after all these years.

The house had been in Ava's family for nearly a century when it became theirs. At one time, it sat on over a hundred and thirty acres of Midwestern farmland. Now, the property line encompassed three acres of overgrown trees and shrubs, the land around him on all sides belonging to a mix of other landlords, none of whom seemed to do anything with the acreage, certainly not farm it. The land made more money in subsidies than it did as a working farm anymore.

The old farmhouse stood alone, a mile from any other structure in any direction. A lost glove on the ground, waiting for someone to find it. It was lonely, befitting Carter, and in a way, he'd grown into the loneliness of the house, the old boards and drafty windows slowly wrapping their arms around him and inviting him into the solitude. Maybe it wasn't himself he talked to out loud, but the house itself.

He found the gun case in a far corner. To the left were the remnants of his own family. Ava's things on the right.

"There you are," he said. "Didn't think I'd be able to find you so easy."

The leather was dry and brittle, in need of a good saddle soap but otherwise solid. It was a deep tan color except for the handle and the area around the zipper where it had been rubbed lighter by his father's hand and his grandfather before him. Not by Carter. When he'd taken the gun in as part of his father's last load of things, it went into the corner and hadn't moved in over twenty years.

Carter hadn't fired a gun since the Army, and even then, only in basic training. He'd never seen combat, spending his brief time in an office at Fort Scott, Kansas, getting out as soon as his obligation was over, then using his GI bill money for college.

He lifted the case and brought it out under the harsh light of the bulb. Felt a little like shaking hands with his dad again to have his palm wrapped around the well-worn handle his father used to hold. He pulled back the zipper, and it stuck about eight inches from the top. He took the whole case downstairs into better light.

"Get this thing unstuck," he muttered.

Carter sprayed some WD-40 on the zipper and got it open. The gun looked like an antique, and he guessed it was at this point. No license. No serial number in a database somewhere. A hand-me-down from father to son and then father to son again.

There was a box of shells, and he opened the brittle cardboard. Seven inside. More than enough. If the gun would fire at all.

He zipped it back inside the case and went to do some research on how to get an old gun in working order again.

It didn't take long to find some alternatives to gun oil. He didn't want to have to go buy the real stuff since that would leave a trail. He planned to kill Justin Lyons, but he also planned to get away with it. Even for a short time. Buying gun supplies out of the blue wasn't the way to do it.

Several gun owner forums, of which he found thousands, said a lightweight motor oil would do the trick. He only needed to get the gun ready enough to fire one shot.

Opening the old gun case made him think of another case he hadn't opened in far too long. He went to the far reaches of the closet in his bedroom and pulled out the black guitar case. He had to shove aside the rack of Ava's clothes still hanging there.

He laid the case on the bed and undid the four hinges then lifted the lid. Nestled in a bed of maroon velvet was an acoustic guitar made of rich mahogany. Another hand-me-down from Dad.

Carter hadn't played since Ava died. He'd never been all that great, but she loved to hear him play. He knew some old blues, some folk songs that made them think of their younger days. He tried to write a song or two back several decades ago but decided to leave it to the professionals.

He lifted the guitar from the case. The wood was well-worn along the top where his arm rested and his father's before that. The back of the neck, where his hand slid up and down, had softened and faded. The strings were tarnished and old, and when he strummed it, they were badly out of tune.

He sat on the edge of the bed and set the guitar on his lap. It felt like an old friend. Felt the way he always wanted a grandchild to feel sitting on his knee.

He turned the tuning peg on the A string and got it where he thought an A might be. He didn't have perfect pitch by any means, but close enough for a lone country house with no audience. He went down the line trying to tune the strings, which had long lost their tone. He got to the B string, second from the bottom, and when he turned the peg, it snapped off in his hand.

He flinched like someone had slapped him. He turned the guitar over and saw that the tiny screws holding the peg in place had corroded and broken in two.

"Well, damn it."

He set the guitar back in the case.

"Another project for tomorrow, I guess."

Restore two old relics. One for making music and one for taking revenge.

A row of unread books sat on the shelf. Carter ran a finger down the line, wondering if it was a good use of his remaining time to finish one or more. And which one would get the honor of being his last? He was two behind in the Hap and Leonard series, about a pair of Texas shit-kickers who get in all sorts of trouble. Funny and exciting both, but he found it hard to get motivated for anything on the shelf.

A pain gripped his abdomen. The same pain that had driven him to the doctor in the first place six months ago, the pain that launched his search for a diagnosis. It started sharp and then spread like ink, dissipating in water. He remained still, bent at the waist, waiting for it to pass. He exhaled slowly, pushing air out through his teeth like a steam line releasing pressure.

Each time the pain grabbed him, it took a few seconds longer to release its grip. Labor pains getting closer to delivery, only his pains drew him closer to death. He bent further over, inhaled another deep breath through his nose, and let it out slowly. The pain faded until he could almost forget he was dying soon.

"Son of a bitch," he said when he had his lungs back. "That was a bad one."

He left the bookshelf behind, no decision made, grabbed the keys to his pickup, and drove away from the house down the rutted and muddy driveway. A full quarter mile before he reached paved road. His red Ford had faded to a burnt orange color, and the frame rattled like dice in a cup, but the engine was solid and caught on the first turn every time. The truck was like Carter—old, but reliable. Weathered, but solid. A worker, one that wouldn't let you down.

The town of Bellington was an in-between place. A stop-over on the way to somewhere else. It was large enough that they didn't have to bus the kids to school in another town, but small enough that there were only two gas stations—one as you entered town and another two miles later as you left. The homes started in a cluster near the center of town and then spread as if land deeds had been scattered in the wind. It made sense nearly all the restaurants in Bellington were drive-throughs.

Those that did stay made a life, though. Like weeds in cracks of asphalt, where the soil is good, roots take hold. Retired, widowed, no children left alive—Carter could have gone anywhere, but he stayed.

He was tired of talking to himself. It only made him realize in stark black and white how few friends he had anymore. It was his own doing. His world had shrunk since Ava died. He wasn't all that old, but most of his friends had already passed. Heart disease, lung cancer, COVID-19. One by one, they all dropped off the map. His lone buddy, Ken, was still with us but had been stuffed away in a nursing home by his kids a few years back.

Carter pulled into the visitor spots at Grand Oak Retirement Village. His was the only car.

The inside smelled antiseptic, the lighting devoid of color and warmth to match the skin tone of the residents. He asked for Ken and was told he was in the Rec Room by a bored-looking receptionist.

Carter walked down the hall, trying not to look into any of the open doors on either side. He heard low moans and deep, chest-rattling coughs from far off. He tried to breathe through his mouth and not his nose. He thanked his stars his disease would take him quickly and not land him in a place like this.

Ken was seated in front of a square table with a five-hundred-piece puzzle on it. So few of the pieces had been assembled, Carter had no idea what the picture was supposed to be.

"Hey there, pal."

Ken looked up. Carter noticed his seat was a wheelchair. When had that happened?

Ken's face broke into a wide smile. His cheeks were stippled with white whiskers, the wrinkles deep set. Brown spots mottled his skin on every exposed surface.

"Heeeeey, there." He drew out his greeting, but Carter noticed he didn't use his name and there was a distance in his eyes. Carter took a folding chair next to Ken.

"How you doin', buddy?"

"Yeah," Ken said. "Hey."

Carter gestured to the puzzle. "You workin' on this?"

Ken waved it away. "Nah."

"Been keepin' busy, though?"

"I guess so. You?"

"Yeah. You bet."

Carter couldn't see past the vacancy in his friend's eyes. "Ken? You remember me, don't you?"

"Sure."

"What's my name?"

"Aw come on."

"Ken. What's my name?"

"Don't gimmie that. I know you."

"Then what's my name?"

Ken kept a smile pasted on his face, but Carter could see the struggle to keep it there.

"Movies," Ken said. "You're in the pictures."

Carter smiled. "Yeah, that's right. You got me."

He decided it didn't matter if Ken didn't know his name anymore. He was in there, buried in some synapse as a vague memory that might have been harder to access but had stayed around when so many others had vanished.

They sat in silence for a while. Carter put his hands in his pockets, wary of touching surfaces, even though everything smelled like bleach. He still hadn't seen a single nurse or orderly since the front desk girl when he arrived.

"Y'know, Ken. I'm thinking about doing something."

"Yeah, sure."

"Something I'm not sure I should do."

19

"Something serious?"

"Yeah. Dead serious."

"Then don't do it."

Carter shook his head. "No, I said that wrong. I think I should do it. Some people don't. Ava wouldn't."

His face brightened again. "Oh, how's Ava?"

It stung like a match tip being pressed to his skin. Ken had been at the funeral, but it seemed Ava's death was lost in the fog somewhere. Carter was momentarily jealous that, in Ken's mind, she was still alive. He saw no reason to have to convince Ken that she was gone. "She's good."

"That's good." Ken settled back in his chair and folded his hands in his lap, listening.

"Ken, this thing I'm thinking of doing…it's to even things out. Set things right again."

Ken nodded. "Mmmh-hmm."

Carter had no idea what Ken understood, figured little, but talking made it better somehow. He did wonder to himself briefly why it was easier to talk to Ken about killing a man than about his own diagnosis and imminent death, which he had chosen not to mention.

"But this thing, it's not a hundred percent legal."

"Aw, what's that matter to us?"

A lucid moment. "Right. That's what I'm thinking. I mean, if I think it needs doing, I should do it, right?"

"Yeah, sure. Why not?"

Because it's killing a man is why not. Carter just smiled. He reached out and patted Ken on his hands. The bones were sharp under papery skin.

"Thanks, pal. You hang in there, okay?"

"Hanging in there."

Carter looked around the room and wondered how he compared to the others. His hair was just as white, his wrinkles nearly as deep. Was it all in the eyes? The awareness, the life. But Carter was aware of his own coming night and aware that he had another man's death on his agenda. Damn, it might be easier to not know what the finished picture looked like. Just take the pieces as they came.

Carter stood. He bent over the table and pushed two pieces of the edge together. Blue. Must be sky. He gave Ken a small wave and avoided looking at any of the others as he left.

He walked back through the lobby. A large orderly in a white shirt and clip-on tie called out to him.

"Where you headed to?"

Carter stopped and turned to him. "My car. Why?"

"Oh, sorry." The man raised his hands in apology. "I thought you were a resident."

Carter forced a smile that only lifted one side of his mouth. "Making a break for it, huh?"

"Yeah. You'd be surprised how many try it."

He gave a quick look around the lobby. "No, I wouldn't." He walked out.

Justin Lyons had been out of prison for twelve years after serving eight of a twelve-year sentence. Carter had been in the courtroom every day for the trial. Ava couldn't bear to attend.

He sat ramrod straight with his eyes focused on every word as if he were transcribing the events in his head. He'd made friends with a woman on the prosecution team, and even though he felt like she took pity on him, he used her sympathies to get information. He knew when Justin was up for parole each time, and he knew when he was released. From there, it hadn't been hard to keep tabs on him.

Justin worked at a restaurant bussing tables in a town about thirty miles from Carter's place. It was a mid-sized town, like most in the Upper Midwest. Nothing you could call a city, but more than one stop light.

He parked across the street from the place. A Greek joint called Spirit of Athens. He settled in to watch the door.

When Ava would plead with him not to go to court, she'd say Audrey's death had been an accident, and obsessing over it wouldn't help.

Carter never argued with her, but politely disagreed and went anyway.

The judge agreed it was an accident of sorts. Negligent homicide is what they called it. Audrey and two other people lay dead in a twist of car parts and glass. The other two, accidents. Audrey, a direct result of Justin Lyons.

People had testified that he kept feeding her drinks. The defense said she was twenty-one and could make her own decisions about how much to drink. A witness said she saw her rebuff Justin's advances. The defense said no evidence of sexual assault was present. A girlfriend said she recalled hearing Audrey specifically say she didn't want to leave with him, but then, when she passed out, multiple people saw Justin carry her to his car and put her in the passenger seat. Those same people all testified to how much Justin had to drink. Two previous DUI arrests didn't help his case. Neither did the two assault charges, and one drunk and disorderly.

Five minutes after leaving the party, he collided head-on with the Millers, an older couple returning from a movie. Justin Lyons was the only one who walked away alive.

He'd limped into the courtroom every day on a cane, but Carter knew it was a prop. He never took the stand, never said a word for himself the whole time. On the final day he read a statement with a mumbled apology. He kept his head down, reading the words as if they were the first time he'd seen them. Carter seethed at the moment more than any other in the trial. More than the stories about how Audrey tried to stay away from him, and he followed her around the party, handing her drinks and refusing to hear her say no.

Carter knew Audrey was partly to blame. He hadn't taught her to drink like that. He enjoyed wine on the weekends, the occasional single malt, but he was never drunk in her presence. But she was newly twenty-one, and that's what kids that age did.

After she passed out, though, everything that happened after Justin Lyons did to her, and for that, he needed to pay. Eight years wasn't nearly enough.

Bargains and deals and backroom agreements between the lawyers meant that DUI charges were dropped and other, smaller charges set aside in favor of the big one, which they talked down to the negligent homicide. After sentencing, the lawyer approached Carter with a smile on his face and a hand out to shake on the victory. Carter merely stared at him, curious how he could think this warranted a celebration.

Carter never figured himself for a killer. He ground his teeth, thinking of the contradiction in his soul. Being so angry at a man for causing a death, and then here he sat, planning a death in a far more calculated way than Justin had.

But the world was out of balance.

And now that he was so close to death himself, he saw how easy dying was. You barely had to do a thing.

A hunched figure came down the sidewalk, hands stuffed in the pockets of a surplus army jacket. He walked with a slight hitch in his step, a little limp that was years old. And his head hung down between his shoulders, focused on the ground in front of him. A prison walk. And the look of a man reading from a sheet of paper, the way Justin had in the courtroom on the day of his sentencing.

Carter sat up straighter, his chest tightening. He hadn't laid eyes on Justin in years. The weight of what he was planning came to a rest on his sternum, and he struggled for breath.

Carter started the truck and pulled away from the curb with a chirp of tires.

He bought some 30-weight motor oil and sat on his back porch, oiling the rifle and watching the sun go down over the unkempt trees. Bats darted across the sky, fast as a blink. A shadow, taken flight.

Carter loaded one shell into the rifle. The wood was worn smooth as only time and a calloused hand could make it. Softer than any sandpaper would do. He was nervous to shoot. The old gun might blow up in his hands. And he had barely fired a gun since he left the Army, only when he obliged his father and tagged along on a hunting trip. Carter was a notoriously bad shot, compared to his dad anyway, but his father had never pushed Carter to kill. They went after wild turkey and rabbit. Carter never hit a rabbit once. Too damn fast. Turkeys were dumb and slow, but Carter would hit them square in the chest and his mom would have to dig out the shot from the breast while she prepared the bird.

He preferred fishing, and his father would take him for long, quiet afternoons on the shore of a lake or in a small aluminum boat. Carter remembered his first confrontation with real death came through fishing. They'd been out for catfish, and Carter, only a boy at the time, spent the ride home poking and playing with the fish in the bucket. Three large catfish with their long whiskers fascinated him.

He followed his father out back to where he had a table set up. Little more than a slab of wood painted battleship grey. There was a lead pipe hanging from a hook and a bucket on one end. His dad took a fish, laid it on the slab, and with no warning to Carter, hit in the head with the pipe. The white belly of the catfish streaked with red from the blood. It took three strikes.

25

Carter stood back in shocked silence as his father beheaded the fish, sliced it down the smooth middle, and gutted it, sliding the entrails down into the empty bucket like it was nothing more than crumbs from a plate. He learned then how average death is. How quickly it passes, and how soon the world moves on.

Carter lifted the gun to his shoulder. He took aim into the woods at nothing in particular. He squeezed the trigger. It took more pull than he expected, but it fired. He knew there'd be a bruise on his shoulder tomorrow and wondered if that would be a giveaway if the police had cause to question him. He sat and listened to the sound of the shot fade in the air around him and wondered if, on the day, the sound would die first or if Justin Lyons would.

The next day, he loaded the guitar case into his car and drove it down to the music store. It was a forty-mile drive, and he thought of songs he might like to learn how to play. Maybe he'd have time to learn one or two. For the first time in a long while, he turned on the radio. None of the songs were familiar, but the sound was like having someone in the seat next to him.

He walked the beat-up old case into the store and laid it on the counter in front of a man in his twenties with a shock of orange hair and a nose ring. Carter was the only customer in the store filled with hanging electric and acoustic guitars on the wall, amplifiers on the floors all around him, a room in back for drums, and posted flyers for lessons on every instrument from saxophone to piano.

"Hey there," the man with orange hair said. "What can I help you with?"

"Well, I got this old boy down out of storage, and one of the tuning pegs has snapped off, it looks like. I'd like to get it repaired."

"Okay, let's take a look."

Another man, this one in his forties with a goatee and a ball cap on his head with a Taylor guitars logo on it, wandered out from the back room, working some food from his teeth with his tongue.

Carter opened the case and made sure it didn't slap down on the glass case.

"Holy shit." The kid with the hair stared at the guitar like Carter had just opened a book of secrets.

"Hey, c'mere, Ed." The kid waved over the older man, who didn't rush getting there. When he did, he had the same reaction. "Holy shit."

The kid looked at Carter. "Can I take it out?"

"Sure." He didn't know what the fuss was.

The kid lifted the guitar out of the case like it was made of glass.

"Dude." He turned it over in his hands, held it out, and stared down the neck like he was a doctor examining a spine. He tapped lightly on the back and sides and finally plucked the A string and let it resonate.

"Beautiful, man."

"Yeah," said Ed, the older man. "Read me that serial number."

They went to work, ignoring Carter. The kid got out a small pen light and peered through the hole. He read off a series of numbers, which the older man entered into a computer. While they waited for whatever he was searching for, the kid turned to Carter.

"This is gorgeous, man. You the original owner?"

"My father."

"Wow."

"I didn't know there was anything special to it."

"Serious? Dude, this guitar is, like, valuable. Like, really valuable."

The older man spoke up, his face still in the computer screen. "It's a nineteen thirty-two."

Carter shrugged. Seemed about right to him. He figured it was old and worn out, though, not a collector's piece.

"Damn," the kid with orange hair said.

Ed came back, and they examined the broken peg. They discussed it in forensic detail.

"I wouldn't want to lose any of the wood here."

"Yeah, just filler should do it."

"Maybe. You know who we need to call?"

"Arlo."

"Yep."

The kid turned back to Carter. "We got a guy who does wood. Really good. A craftsman. I'd want him to take a look. The peg is fine. Needs new screws, but I bet Arlo could save all the original wood. It's just the little screw holes, and not much else is damaged. You took good care of this, man."

28

"Thanks. So when you say valuable…?"

The men traded a look. Orange hair said, "Ten grand? Low end, maybe. I mean, you'd do better in a big city. Find the right collector, and you could really make out. You thinking of selling?"

He looked at Carter like a hungry man eyeing a steak.

"No. Just curious."

"Just don't put it in Ebay, please, man. If you wanna sell it, bring it back here. We'll make you a good deal."

"Okay. Gotta get it fixed first, though."

"Yeah, yeah. I'll get my guy on it and get it done right away. You okay to leave it here?"

"Sure."

"Let me make you out a receipt."

Carter smiled at the men and the reverence they had for an old instrument he'd nearly forgotten about. He thanked them and left the two men to stare at the old guitar nestled in its case where it had slept for years.

Carter knew he was procrastinating, sitting there outside the restaurant waiting for Justin's shift to end. He hadn't even brought the gun.

"A little reconnaissance," he told himself.

The truck still smelled like fried chicken. A takeout bag was crumpled on the seat next to him. He burped and felt a tightening in his gut. Could be the chicken, but he knew better. Nine-syllable name or not, Carter knew what lived inside him. A black ball of hate that had been growing malignant for more than twenty years. The doctors could call it what they wanted, but it was the festering anger and his inability to do anything about it for decades that led to his final exit being weeks, not years, away.

In many ways, it was his own fault. Ava had told him to let it go. Not to forget. Never forget Audrey. But let go of the hate. Carter had to wonder, though, if her own heart had been so broken that it killed her. A year later, ten years later, did it matter? Some wounds never heal.

Justin stepped out the front door of The Spirit Of Athens and tucked his hands in the front pockets of his jeans. He walked, head down, to his car, and Carter followed. Justin lived only ten minutes from the restaurant in a house Carter didn't think he could afford. Probably a rental. Maybe he had roommates. That would make his task harder, but there were no other cars in the driveway. No movement within the house.

He drove a four-door Toyota, which had its share of dings and rust spots. A used car if Carter ever saw one. Tires slightly bald, the back half of the word Camry was missing, so it just said Cam on the trunk.

Carter slowed and parked across the street and watched as Justin went

30

inside his house and went about his life. The simple things Audrey could not do.

So he knew where Justin Lyons lived now. Knew how to find him and follow him. It was all he needed to do what he promised himself he would. He tried to imagine it for a minute, tried to play it out in his head so when it really happened, he wouldn't panic. But he couldn't see it. No image would come. It was so far removed from anything in his real life he had no imagination to even put pictures to the thoughts.

Carter drove away and didn't look back.

He couldn't call it an impulse because he'd been thinking about it quietly for a while, so when he pulled into the animal shelter, he wondered what had taken him so long.

"Let's see what we got here."

Carter went inside and said to the girl behind the desk with straight black hair and chipped nail polish, "I want to see the oldest dog you got."

She blinked at him twice and then slid off her stool. "You really do?"

"Yep. Older the better."

"Mister, it's your lucky day."

She walked him down the row of chain link pens where dogs sounded off like alarm bells, some begging to be taken home, some warning him away. She stopped and waved a bored hand at the last pen in the row.

"This is Chester. He was a surrender about eight months ago. Owner died, and the kids didn't want him."

Carter looked through the diamond pattern of the fencing and into the red-veined eyes of a coon hound with enough gray in the fur around his muzzle that he looked like he stuck his face into a vat of flour. The old boy was sitting, one leg thrown out to the side. He stood, and it looked like he might not make it on the first try, but he managed. He moved slowly to the door, and if his joints had creaked like an old back porch door, it would have sounded entirely fitting.

Chester put his nose in one of the holes and sniffed.

Carter bent down on his own creaky knees and rubbed the snout.

"Hey, boy. How you doing today?"

Chester chuffed and stuck his tongue through the fence to lick Carter's hand.

"We don't know how old he is," the girl said. "But old."

"Yeah, I can see that. Chester, you say?"

"Yeah. We give them names that start with the same letter as their breed, and since he's a coon hound, he's a c-h and so, Chester."

Carter stood. "I'd say he's about perfect."

Carter filled out paperwork, paid a fee, and made an extra donation to the shelter. The girl brought Chester out on a leash.

"You know he doesn't have long, right?"

Carter took the leash from her. "Darling, none of us do."

Chester had an extra spring in his step as they went out to Carter's truck. Carter had to lift him into the passenger seat, but when he positioned himself with his back leaning on the seat and his gray muzzle facing the wide world outside the window, he sat like the king on his throne. Carter rolled the window down halfway and let Chester get some wind in his jowls on the way home.

"We're gonna have a good time, you and me. No more cages."

Carter had a hard time getting the grin off his face when he looked at the dog. The old boy was just happy to be alive and out of that prison. Didn't take much to get his tail wagging. Carter kept reaching over and scratching behind Chester's ears, which made the dog grumble in pleasure. He needed a bath and to be fattened up some, but he was perfect.

When they got to the farmhouse, Carter helped him down out of the truck, then let him have a run at the yard. Chester didn't move fast, and his nose worked harder than his legs. After ten minutes of vacuuming up every smell he could in a circle around the house, Carter led him up the steps as the sun went down and invited the old coon hound into his house.

"It's yours now as much as mine. Make yourself at home."

Chester wasted no time. He was snoring on the couch by the time Carter had gotten out of the bathroom. He realized he hadn't bought any dog food. He threw a pound of ground beef in a pan and made them both a plate of meat and bread. The smell roused the dog off the couch, and he stood by

Carter's feet, tail slapping the cabinets. Carter set the bowl on the floor next to him at the kitchen table and laughed as Chester made almost sexual sounds of pleasure, slurping up the meat.

"Chester, you and me are gonna get along just fine."

For two weeks he sat and watched and followed Justin Lyons. Chester snored by his side in the cab of the truck. He seemed to like getting out and riding along with Carter. Already, he was attached to the old man's hip.

"Between the two of us," Carter said with a scratch to Chester's ears, "we almost make one good hip." He chuckled and imagined Chester would have, too, if he could.

In his time watching Justin, he hadn't seen much of the man's life. No girlfriend he could tell, no real friends. He never went out drinking or out to eat beyond stopping on his way home for a burger or a taco. He limped from home to work and back home with occasional trips to the post office. Too many trips to the post office, but that was his business. Maybe he sold vintage baseball cards online. Who knew?

Justin's life seemed small and monotonous. It almost gave Carter sympathy for him, but then he'd stop and think of all the mundane things Audrey never got to do. Waiting for the dryer to be done at the laundromat. Balancing a checkbook with nothing in it. Watching a TV show you've already seen three times. Replacing a lightbulb. Filling the car with gas. All those ordinary moments his daughter never got to see. No matter how small and pathetic Justin Lyons' life was, it was still a life.

"It don't seem fair, does it?"

Chester grunted and adjusted himself on the seat, then went right on sleeping.

Chester wasn't much for fetch. He was more of an all-sniff-all-the-time dog when he wasn't napping, which was most of the time.

Carter went out and got a case of canned dog food, the good stuff with gravy that was probably mostly horse meat, but Chester didn't care. He scarfed it down like they were all Kentucky Derby winners.

"Good, huh, boy?" He patted Chester's haunches. "We eat like kings from here on out. No need to count calories or watch our weight."

His heavy tail slapped against Carter's leg whenever he would slide up next to the dog and scratch him behind the ears. Chester looked at him with his droopy eyes as if they had been roommates for decades already. They were each other's missing piece and they settled into the comfort of two old hounds easily. Best of all, Carter no longer felt silly talking out loud to an empty room. Even if Chester couldn't answer back, his words had more purpose. And really, who doesn't talk to their dog? He hadn't gone as far as to answer himself in a high-pitched dog voice, but Chester would have more of a baritone anyway if Carter thought about it, which he hadn't. Not much, anyway.

Carter lifted the dog into the cab of the truck, and Chester waited for the window to be rolled down. They drove to Red Hills cemetery. Carter led him on a leash, keeping an eye out for the caretaker in case Chester felt like lifting his leg on any tombstones. He could jerk the leash and tell him to save it until no one could see.

They stopped at a side-by-side plot. Audrey McCoy in one spot, Ava McCoy in the other, and a blank space on the stone next to Ava's name.

36

Carter thought maybe they should go ahead and put his name there and the born on date to save time down the road.

Chester laid down on the grass over Ava and started snoring. The sound reminded Carter of his wife. She could saw logs like a lumberjack in her sleep.

He faced Audrey.

"I'm going to do a thing." He turned his eyes to the grass. "I don't know if it's something you'd approve of. I know your mother wouldn't. But it's something I gotta do. I'm doing it for me, yes, but also for you."

He let a long moment pass while he pushed down the emotion welling in his throat.

"I don't have much time left, so I guess that's lit a fire under my ass. I don't know if I'll feel better afterward or not. I guess I'll find out. All I do know is that while you're laying here under dirt that freezes and thaws and grass that dies and comes back, while you get rained on and snowed on and people walk over you to get to some other name they know on down the row, that man can't keep on living. He don't deserve the sun you can't see."

He turned slightly to face Ava.

"I know you'd think this is foolish and that I should let it go. But I can't. When that doctor told me what I'm up against...I knew what had to be done. You'll say it's a man's foolish pride and you may be right. But I think it's setting things to right again. They've been out of whack too long. I can't blame all the world's problems on what happens in our little town, but my world ain't been right since that night he loaded her into his car. And my world is the only one I know. And it's worth something. Worth more than he has a right to spoil. He's had more than twenty years more than her. That's enough in my book. More than he earned in his life."

He sniffed, rubbed the tip of his nose with the back of his hand.

"I hope you won't be mad at me if I see you again. It's a risk, I know. But you been mad at me before, lord knows. We always made it through. But either way, I'll see you soon. Unless I don't. In which case it won't matter one way or the other what I do."

Carter looked out over the uneven rows of stones, whites, and grays, square and rounded, crosses and solid blocks. Some taller, like it matters in a place like this to stand out.

"Anyways, I love you both. I miss you like hell." He waved a hand down to the dog. "Oh, this is Chester. He's my buddy. He farts, and he snores, and he craps bigger than he looks like he would, but he's a good boy. You'd like him."

He rousted Chester, who stood slowly and with a grunt. They walked back down the rows, moving deliberately. Carter read the names, looked at the dates. Chester stopped to sniff at a grave where the grass hadn't grown in yet.

They got back to the truck, and Carter loaded Chester inside.

"Well, boy, I guess there's nothing left to do but to do it."

The gun bag leaned against the seat where Carter had gotten used to seeing Chester. The dog was at home, not invited on this trip. He'd lifted his head from the couch cushion and watched Carter leave. Carter couldn't look him in the eye, or he felt he'd have the need to explain it to him, and he wasn't sure he could.

He drove to Justin Lyons' street and parked a few doors down where he could see the house clearly. Today was Justin's late shift, so the street would be quiet and dark by the time he got home. The house directly across the street was vacant, or at least Carter had never, in all his surveillance, seen a light on or a soul around. The house next door on the left was behind a chainlink fence and some high, unruly bushes. The place on the right had no fence, no bushes. Nothing but a sharp contrast in the two lawns where they met—Justin's being brown and weedy and the other being green but overlong.

All he'd ever seen from that house was the glow of a TV in the windows.

He'd thought a few times about the possibility it might be best to shoot himself after he shot Justin, but now he had Chester, so that idea was out. Settling this score was no longer the last thing on his checklist.

He'd gotten his guitar back with another offer that if he ever wanted to sell, he should come back to them. He thanked them for the woodwork—you truly couldn't tell where the repair had been made—and took the guitar home to learn a few songs.

He tried out Johnny Cash's *Ring Of Fire* first, then Buck Owens' *Act Naturally*. They sounded good on the old instrument, but not on his voice.

Didn't matter, though. Who was going to hear him? Chester didn't seem to mind when the old man warbled. He wanted to try some James Taylor next. Carter was trying to decide which song to learn when he saw Justin pull into his driveway.

A sudden cramp seized his gut. He had no idea if it was his disease or his nerves. Seeing Justin now, knowing there was a loaded weapon next to him, made Carter wonder if he really had it in him to kill. He could make that Justin's last car ride. His last everything.

He bent over and set his head against the steering wheel and breathed deep, hoping the cramp would pass, also hoping it wouldn't, and he could drive away and blame his rotten insides.

But it did pass. And with his eyes closed, he saw Audrey, forever frozen at twenty-one. For her. Do this for her. No amount of suffering was too much for him. He had it easy.

Carter rolled down the window and let a light breeze inside the cab. He realized he'd been sweating when the cool air hit his skin. A light came on inside Justin's place. Did he have any weapons of his own in there? Would he come to the door with a pistol in his hand?

And what if Carter got right to the precipice and couldn't pull the trigger?

He had to find out.

He reached over and unzipped the gun case. He slid out the rifle, and the truck filled with the smell of motor oil. A single shell was already loaded inside. Carter had another in his pocket in case, but he surely didn't know if he'd be able to reload and shoot again. It was going to take all seventy-plus years of his courage to fire once.

"For Audrey. Do it for her."

He scanned the street. No motion, no cars. A quiet suburban night.

Carter got out and shut the door quietly behind him. No sense alerting nosy neighbors that someone was around. He held the gun in his right hand, no way to conceal it. His fingers were gripped into the lever-action handle. He stood by his truck for a long moment, running his tongue along the inside of his mouth to try to get some moisture going.

He forced a picture into his mind of Audrey on the table at the morgue.

Her features twisted, and her hair pasted down with dried blood. It wasn't his daughter, not anymore. Justin Lyons had stolen her away. Away from her parents, away from the world.

Carter put one foot down, then another. He was across the street without thinking. He palmed sweat off his forehead and stepped onto the walkway to Justin's door. Cracks in the cement slabs all grew weeds like missed spots while shaving.

He lifted the gun and set the wooden grip in his left hand. His right still gripped tight to the stock, his index finger far away from the trigger.

He reached the door and stopped. So many times he'd thought about this. None of those fantasies got it right. They were missing the sting of sweat in his eyes, the shortness of breath, the smell of motor oil.

His right hand came off the gun and knocked on the door, three hard raps. He hefted the gun again, this time placing his finger on the trigger. He held it down by his hips. No bruise on his shoulder this time.

Carter could feel his heart speeding up. He wondered if Ava had felt her heart clanging against her ribs during her attack.

"Dammit, hurry up."

He pictured Audrey on her high school graduation. He pictured her gravestone. He remembered the casket being lowered and every day in court when Justin sat stone silent and unapologetic, his lawyer arguing that enough people had lost their lives in the accident that was nobody's fault. To send this young man to prison would be to add to that total.

The door opened. Carter could see the beginnings of wrinkles around Justin's eyes. Hard eyes, lines earned through worry and fear—not laughter.

Carter had thought of a million things to say in that moment. When it came to it, he saw Justin's eyes go wide at recognizing the gun, if not the man behind it.

"Audrey McCoy," was all he said. So he would know.

Carter fired. The close range opened up a bloom of red on Justin's chest, and he jumped back as if punched by an unseen fist. The shot looked dead center of his heart. Carter knew he didn't have to reload. The sound seemed louder here than it had in his backyard, and he knew he needed to go.

He gave one look to Justin, who lay on his back, unmoving on the hardwood floor. Carter watched as the body sank an inch, as if melting into the floor, but Carter knew it was the last breath leaving his lungs. The job was done. He turned to go.

As his head swiveled, he saw the house next door on the right. The unobstructed view. A girl stood on the porch staring at him with frightened eyes, one hand on the screen door, bare feet, and a scream caught in her throat.

TWO

Carter McCoy had a decision to make: Kill the witness or not?

They stood facing each other, neither one moving. He could feel a mosquito buzz past his ear. The girl kept one hand on the screen door. She couldn't have been more than eighteen, he figured. Her carrot-orange hair was trimmed close to her head in a pixie cut. She wore short-legged overalls covering an oversized t-shirt. Her feet were bare as if she'd just stepped outside for a moment of fresh air, but found herself in the wrong moment.

Carter would have to reload the gun. She'd see it and run inside, and then he'd have to chase her. He could hear the TV blaring through the open door, so he guessed somebody else was inside. She was too young to live on her own in a three-bedroom house. The whole thing was a risk, but more of a risk than leaving her to identify him?

He kept taking slow, even breaths and saw by the rise and fall of her shoulders that their breathing was in sync.

Killing Justin was one thing; killing an innocent girl was entirely something else. He let the gun barrel drop to face the boards of the porch. He took a tentative step toward the street. She might be able to describe him. Pretty well, now that they had been staring at each other for so long. But that was okay. He did what he did. If they needed to throw him in jail for the last few months of his life, so be it. The girl would live.

He kept his body facing hers and took the three steps down off the porch. She kept still, her eyes moving with him as he made his slow retreat. He watched her the whole way to his truck, always expecting she would pull out a cell phone that everyone her age had and snap a photo of him.

He reached the truck and tossed the gun on the seat before pulling himself into the cab. The girl hadn't moved, hadn't taken her hand off the screen door. Carter started the truck and pulled away slowly from the curb. Tearing his eyes away from hers felt like letting go of a rope that was holding him from falling into a bottomless black.

Breanna let out a long breath. Her mouth was dry, and she still didn't fully trust what her eyes had shown her. The sound had snapped her head around, and she saw the old man on the porch of that weird neighbor, Justin. It was clear the old man had just fired the gun.

Justin's door hung open, and light spilled out onto the porch, but she couldn't see inside from her own porch. She debated walking over there to check on what really had happened, but she didn't want to know. Whatever that was, it was their business.

Bree pulled open the screen door to her house with a squeak and went inside.

Her mama, as usual, was in her comfy chair, TV on, and a tray next to her with the remnants of more than one meal on it. Mama spilled over the sides of the chair, all three hundred-plus pounds of her. Bree judged by the greasy strings of her hair that she had gone more than a few days without showering. Again.

She didn't look worried, wasn't craning her neck to see next door. Had she not heard the shot? With the volume of the TV, Bree could see how she might not have, or how it blended in with the show like a sound effect. Bree started to doubt if she heard it right.

"Where the hell you been?" Mama said. Her voice reminded Bree of a crow's tuneless caw.

"Work," she said.

Bree had nearly perfected the one-word response when talking with her mother. Not much the old lady ever said warranted more. This house was a roof over a three-bedroom coffin, and Bree aimed to dig herself out before too long.

"You get paid today?" Mama had to shout over the TV, which played a game show. Mama wasn't smart enough to know the answers to.

"No, Mama. Friday. Remember?"

Bree knew her mama didn't have a need for days of the week. She survived on government checks and the money Bree's brother gave her.

As much as this joke of a family disgusted and humiliated her, Bree debated telling Mama about what she'd seen, but the giant woman's focus was already back on the TV screen once Bree announced she hadn't come bearing cash in hand. She decided to keep it to herself, doubt creeping along the edges of her brain. She debated walking over there to check it out, see for herself what that old man left behind next door. But if that neighbor guy was dead, she didn't want to see it. And she didn't want to get involved and have to call the cops and answer why she didn't stop the guy. The police wouldn't understand that she thought the old man's eyes looked kind, even from way over on her porch. She didn't want anything to delay her escape from this town, and being a witness to murder would tie her here when all she wanted was to be cut free.

She'd already eaten and so bypassed the kitchen for her bedroom in the back of the house, where she could shut the door and plan for a better life than this. Her brother came through the door to his room. Six foot two and skinny as a straw, Chris play-acted at being a tough guy and a gangster when he was still the kid who got shoved off the playground swings and forced to eat mud. He'd dyed his own orange hair an oil-slick black and wore gold chains over thrift store t-shirts and put two hundred dollar shoes over socks with holes in them.

Bree flinched when she saw him, which made Chris smile. He pulled a set of earbuds out, his chance of hearing the shot obliterated in a hail of gangster rap lyrics from the nineteen nineties.

"I scare you?"

She ignored him and tried to push past to her room. He blocked her way.

"The fuck you going?"

"My room."

"You ain't even gonna eat with the family?"

"I already ate at work."

"That's right, they give you free shit. Why don't you ever bring none home for us?"

She kept her eyes down on the carpet, a dirty green like the whole house was covered in mold. "I only get one burger per shift."

"Yeah, but, you could pocket a few, right? They ain't gonna miss them."

"I don't want to get fired."

He scoffed and waved a hand in front of her. "Fuck 'em. You come work for me."

She shoved him aside, and he laughed as she went by. Torturing his little sister had been Chris's favorite game since Breanna was born. He was Olympic-level. But soon, she'd be gone, and he'd rot away in this town and this house just like Mama.

Bree slammed the door and flopped on the bed, her free after-work burger sitting in her stomach like she'd eaten a cheese-covered pool ball. She thought about the old man next door. The gun, the weird look when he saw her watching him, the red truck. The license plate.

Bree reached over to her small nightstand and scribbled the number down on a page in her journal.

Chester greeted Carter by lifting his head, thumping his tail twice on the sofa cushions, and then snorting before laying back down. Carter set the guncase next to the door and stood there for a while. He couldn't eat, he knew that. In a daze, he walked to the kitchen and poured himself a glass of whiskey. He'd had the bottle for two years now. Never was a big drinker. He looked at the remaining three inches in the bottle and figured he might polish it off tonight.

Chester came padding in with the hope of food showing in the line of drool hanging off his jowls. He pressed his head against Carter's leg, and Carter reached down to scratch his ears.

"I'd ask you if you want one, but..." He lifted his glass to the dog, then drank the rest in one shot. He shivered as it went down. The shakes from the liquor gave way to a full-body spasm as the weight of what he'd done hit him. He nearly dropped the glass as he stood and shook. Chester gave a short whine, knowing something was wrong.

"What did I do, Chester? What did I do?"

He didn't finish the bottle. Carter sat on the couch with one floor lamp on, casting more shadow than light around the room. He stared at nothing while giving Chester a thorough massage to keep his hands doing something.

He ran over the night in his mind. The feel of the trigger on his finger, the crashing sound of the shot. The way Justin fell backward, like he knew he wasn't going to get up again. Then, the girl next door, the way she stared at him. Carter expected to hear sirens any time now.

As much as his thoughts tornadoed around his head, they always returned to Audrey.

"For you. I did it for you."

What would come next, he barely knew. He didn't want to think about songs to learn or goodbyes to say before the disease took him. He wanted to know if he'd be in jail when he passed, or if he'd live long enough to accept what he'd done.

But it was done. No going back now. Too many things in life happened so quick, and time never bothered to slow down or run in reverse. Just as Audrey was taken in an instant as Ava fell to her knees and never stood again. All his planning and following came down to a trigger pull the length of a blink. And now he was a killer.

He rubbed Chester's ear between his fingers, and the dog responded with a low grumble of satisfaction.

"Can I be a good man who did a bad thing?" Carter chuckled lightly. "Jesus, that describes everyone I ever met and everyone who ever took a breath on this earth. Don't let 'em fool you, Chester. Humans are rotten and evil, and they hide it under such love and beauty that we're all fooled too damn easy."

If there was anything seventy-two years taught him, it was that basic truth.

"You dogs do it right. Unconditional love or throat-tearing hate. Ain't no in-between with a dog. They'll either love you or kill you, and you can see each one coming. Not like people who'll smile while they stab you in the back."

He stared at an empty spot on the wall.

"At least I looked him in the eye. That's worth something anyway."

Carter sat in the dim light until he fell asleep sitting up. He didn't want to disturb Chester, who seemed quite comfortable with his head on Carter's lap as if he knew the old man needed a little extra comfort tonight.

Bree had to tell someone about what she'd seen, or thought she saw, and the person she told everything in the world to was Katy. She left the house with Mama asleep in front of the TV, playing a show about doctors. Chris had gone out the way he always did after the sun went down, like some kind of vampire who slept until noon and could use a good tan.

Bree drove her dying Civic hatchback, figuring each trip would be its last. She made it to Katy's and patted the hood when she got out to thank the car for making the journey. She needed the old gal to hold on a little longer so she could get out of this town. Bree had plans, and Katy was part of them. Plans to get out of Bellington and move to California to start over. Her dream was the two of them packed up in this car on life support headed West and even if they broke down as long as it was outside city limits and far enough away she couldn't hear Mama's voice anymore, she'd be fine with that.

She knocked twice on Katy's window and didn't wait for an invitation before sliding the windowpane up, putting one foot on the hose spout, and pushing into Katy's room the way she'd been doing for years now. She almost never came to the front door, especially at night, because Katy's dad was an asshole. Both girls had called him much worse behind closed doors. When he was in the room, it was better to not say anything at all.

She didn't get the usual happy greeting from her best friend, who was always in a good mood no matter what. Bree knew right away why.

Katy was on her bed. She lifted her head and looked toward Bree, but didn't seem to focus on her. Her head seemed loose like a bobblehead doll, and when Katy saw Bree, she laid back down. She was high again.

Most kids around there, either from boredom or the need to put down some hidden pain, had at least tried some of the bathtub meth or the cut-sixteen-ways Mexican heroin that was as easy to get as a can of Mountain Dew from the 7-Eleven. A lot of kids got hooked off their own parent's Oxy stash, and they smoked weed like it would give them clear skin and a college scholarship. Katy had been experimenting. Not an addict…yet. But she had taken that off-ramp. With her dad the way he was, the abuse he put her and her mom through, Bree knew the reason Katy would want to blot out the pain, but when she saw her best friend like this, it broke her heart.

Bree kept clean and kept her eyes on the road out of town. Katy was going to come with her. They had plans. Plans Katy's new habit was not going to fuck up.

She'd been lured, and Bree knew by who. Cash Money, he called himself, or C-Money for shorter and stupider. A sweet talker, a liar, and a predator. A man who excelled in getting younger and younger kids hooked. A man who Bree knew wanted to fuck Katy, too. Bree would rather her do the meth instead.

Bree tried to get Katy to sit up.

"What the fuck, Katy?"

Katy started to cry. "I'm sorry. Shit, I'm sorry, Bree. I know, I know, I know."

When she finally opened her eyes, the pupils were as big as pennies. Bree didn't know what she was on exactly, but did it even matter? She was ruining their plans, spending their money. Katy was becoming more unreliable than the old Civic.

"Was it him again?"

"It was free. I swear, Bree. I didn't spend any of the stash. It was free."

Katy could barely keep her head up or her eyes open. Tears ran down her face.

Bree gave up the idea of telling her about the old man next door and the gun and the shot she heard. She held Katy in her arms and let her best friend sob on her shoulder.

"I'll stop. I promise I'll stop."

"I know," Bree said. But she knew it was a lie. There were people out there grooming Katy to be a customer, waiting for the moment when she couldn't pay in cash and had to submit to other forms of payment. Cruel people who didn't care about anything but money and themselves.

Katy mumbled some words Bree didn't understand, and the tears kept flowing. She wanted so little and so much from the world. She wanted the simple act of getting free from this town and her family and the impossible act of tearing out the roots as she left and expecting them not to grow back. She was a backwoods girl destined to stay that way if her world kept pushing down on her the way it had always done. She'd never get far from the same dirt that clung under her fingernails. Not unless something big happened.

The money was piling up too slowly. The hands that held her down were too strong—her mama, Chris, her bosses, her high school diploma, and nothing else. She needed her own man on a porch with a rifle to blast away the chains binding her here.

She stayed holding Katy until the girl fell asleep with loud snores. Then she held her a little longer.

.

No police came that night. Carter slept on the couch with Chester and woke with a stiff neck. The gun case sat by the door where he'd left it, watching him. He felt the cold stare and knew he had to get it out of his sight in case he was tempted to turn the rifle on himself. He moved the gun case from beside the front door and put it in the closet next to his guitar.

He fed Chester and then let him out the back door to go sniff at the scent trails left by all the nocturnal animals. The sun was barely over the horizon, and Carter stood there, watching it burn the dew off the tall grass and thinking how this would be a new day Justin wouldn't see.

He wondered if he'd been found yet. His plan had been to close the door, leave no trace behind other than the dead body, but that girl had thrown him. Anyone walking by could see the bottoms of Justin's feet. A wandering dog could get curious about the smell. At some point, the mailman would stop by.

Chester's patience for sniffing knew no bounds, and Carter sat out on the back porch with a glass of water and watched him for over an hour. The day brightened into a clear, cloudless morning. Carter felt competing weights press down on him and lift off at the same time. The lightness in Justin being gone and justice finally being served gave way to the ten-ton crush of his disease and the possibility the police could find him.

He'd done a bad thing, and he knew that. He also knew it wasn't a wrong thing. How could he explain that to the law, though? Maybe a jury would see it his way. He knew better. Killing is killing, and the worst part of the feeling is worrying that now he was no better than Justin himself.

"C'mon, boy. You 'bout sniffed the green right off the grass by now."

Chester took his time walking a zig-zag back to the house. He followed Carter inside and found the couch for his mid-morning nap.

Carter looked at his row of books again. Most about murder and death. He didn't have the stomach for it. He went to the cabinet with Ava's jigsaw puzzles. Paintings of snow-covered bridges, horses pulling sleighs, spring flowers, geese in flight. Pleasant images that reminded him what a bright presence Ava was in his life. He shut the cabinet, having no appetite for darkness or light.

He went upstairs and climbed in bed.

Carter woke well past noon. He was hungry and ran some water through his hair to get it to lie down, went downstairs to wake Chester, and walked the dog out to the car. He drove to Mesa Grande. It was the tail end of the lunch rush, and many of the tables were full. He couldn't deal with people, so he decided to get an order to go.

Ivana smiled when she saw him come in.

"Hello there," she said. She was already writing on her order pad. "Sit anywhere you like, Carter."

"Can't stay," he said. "Just give me a usual and also a beef burrito. No beans, no rice. Just beef, and that's all."

She smiled and cocked her head a bit. "Something for later?"

"Nah." He flicked a thumb over his shoulder. "I got a dog."

"Oh, you did?" She peered around him, trying to get a look.

"Yeah. Old and ugly, just like me. We make quite a pair."

She waved a hand at him. "Oh, stop it."

Ivana's teenage daughter came out from the back carrying a plate in each hand. She was rushing and blew a long strand of hair out of her eyes with a swift puff of air. She looked tired, working harder than any kid her age should have to.

"Carter got a dog," her mother told her.

"Oh yeah?"

She didn't stop to chat about it. She kept moving toward the table, waiting for their order. As she whisked past him, he saw under that falling lock of hair the purple skin around her eye. Carter went rigid. Ivana could see him react, and the pleasant smile fell from her face.

"What happened?" he asked her.

"It's nothing." Ivana dropped her voice low. "We appreciate what you did, but things don't change that easy."

Carter watched her deliver the food, trying to force a smile for the customers while keeping her hair covering one eye.

"Eddie?"

"It's not so bad."

Her face could barely conceal the lie. Even if he hadn't known her well, he'd know the bruise on her daughter hurt Ivana just as much.

"He here?" Carter asked.

"No." Ivana's eyes shifted quickly to the kitchen door. The flick of a hummingbird wing, but he saw it.

"I'll get started on your order," she said. "You want a Coke while you wait?"

"No, thanks."

She tore off the order ticket and set it on the pile with the others, then went into the kitchen.

Carter thought about the gun case. About how it was a solution to problems. About how no police showed up. About how only one finger was needed to pull that tiny trigger. He walked outside and opened the passenger door to the truck. He let Chester nuzzle into his neck, then lifted the old dog down and let him sniff the edges of the parking lot. Carter led him around the side, tugging at his leash to get him to move on from particularly good smells until they reached the back of Mesa Grande. Chester became wild with the smells of cooking beef and pork. Equally as fascinating were the garbage cans and large dumpster.

Carter edged closer to the fence surrounding the back area. The gate was open, and now Carter sniffed the wind. He found a smell above the chili and the carne asada—cigar smoke.

He let Chester lead him through the gate. He saw the cigar butt in an ashtray by the back door. No Eddie. He peered around the door jamb into the back of the restaurant. The salsa music muted the kitchen sounds.

Eddie passed by the doorway, pushed open the screen, and picked up the half-spent cigar before he noticed Carter there. He jumped when he saw the dog.

The two men stood still, looking at each other, wondering which might do something foolish first.

"I seen her eye," Carter said. "I want you to know—I'm coming for you."

"You don't understand."

The bravado of the other night was gone from Eddie. Maybe it was the dog, but Chester wasn't anything you could call intimidating.

"I don't think you understood our last conversation. I told you if you laid hands on either of those women again, there was gonna be trouble. Well, son, now you got trouble."

Eddie puffed out his chest in at least a show of toughness. "What do you think you can do to me?"

"Boy, I can do anything I damn well want to you. I'm out of time, and I'm out of worries. Rest of my life is making things right again where they went out of whack. You're my next project."

Inside, a bell rang. Order up. Carter walked away, tugging Chester behind him, who didn't want to leave the wonderland of smells behind.

Carter tied Chester off to the railing, went inside, and paid. "Thank you, Ivana."

"Oh, is that your dog?" She watched Chester scratch at his ears with a creaky back paw.

"Yeah, that's him. Chester."

"He looks sweet."

"Don't let looks fool you. He's a killer." He lifted his bag of food with a nod. "Take care now. Both of you."

"We will."

Carter stopped mid-turn. "Daughters," he said before swallowing, keeping the words from catching in his throat, "are a precious gift. You do whatever you can to protect them because you never want to know what it's like to live if you fail them."

He turned and walked out just as he saw tears brimming in Ivana's eyes. She knew the story. First from rumors and gossip when Carter and Ava would leave the restaurant and people would get to talking. Then, from the couple themselves, the first time they met Ivana's daughter. Ava had talked of Audrey with a smile and fond remembrance. Carter had turned brooding and darker, unable to accept the loss in their lives the way his wife did. Ivana saw the pain in both of them. The bright façade of a mother covering her grief and the dark cloud that followed a father after the unthinkable happened.

Carter untied Chester's leash, and the dog followed with his nose pressed against the bag of food.

"Sounded like a goddamn greeting card, but it's the damn truth."

He lifted Chester into the cab, removed the foil from the burrito, and let Chester have at it right there on the seat.

Bree came out of her room in bare feet, trying to pad silently to the bathroom. It was before ten, so most likely, nobody else was awake. Chris's door opened, and his arm shot across the hall and made a bar across the narrow space.

"Morning, sunshine."

His breath stank. He wore a black t-shirt with a logo for a band she didn't recognize and boxer briefs that had lost most of the elastic around the waist.

"Can you move?"

"I just need to take a piss. Wanted to get there before you because who knows how long you might take."

"Oh, come on, Chris."

"I'll take ten seconds."

"Whatever."

He lifted his arm and put a wide, fake smile on his face. "Thanks, sis!"

Mama had never confirmed if they were full or half-siblings. Bree hadn't followed up because the less she had to think about Mama's sex life, the better. Whoever her father or his was, he hadn't stayed around long enough for a paternity test.

Chris passed her and shut the door to the bathroom with a sharp crack. Bree moved on down the hall to the kitchen. Mama was in the living room, still in her chair, asleep. Bree opened a cabinet and got out the can of Folgers. It was nearly empty, but she could scrape enough to get one cup. She tilted the can to the side, and it slipped and crashed to the floor.

Mama snorted and sat up in her chair.

"Jesus Christ, I thought we got hit by a meteor."

Bree looked at her as she bent to pick up the can. Coffee grounds were spilled across the floor, and the linoleum was dirty enough that sweeping them up and reusing them wasn't an option.

"You thought a meteor hit the house?"

"There was a big bang."

Bree held out the Folgers can. "We're out of coffee."

"Well, shit. You get paid today?"

"You got money. You don't need me buying you coffee."

Mama grunted. "Fine."

She pulled the lever on the side of the Lay-Z-Boy and sat up straighter. Bree thought she might get out of the chair for a moment, but Mama only pointed to her purse hanging off one of the chairs at the table.

"Get a twenty out of there and get me some dip, too."

"Are you serious? Always bitching about money, and you're gonna spend it on dip?"

"Don't give me shit, little girl."

On a long list of bad habits, it was her worst. The old Pepsi bottle next to the chair filled near to the rim with a brown swirl of spit and tobacco juice. Bree took the twenty and wondered if she added it to her stash, would Mama even remember later on that she didn't get her coffee. The coffee, maybe. The dip? No way.

Bree looked down the hall. Bathroom door, still closed. She sighed, pulled a beanie over her red hair, and walked out the door.

She walked around to the side of the house and pulled down her pants. She squatted near the bushes overgrown outside her bedroom window. She had a clear view of the house next door, and when she was finished, she walked slowly to the edge of the property. She stepped from overgrown but green grass to short and brown. There were no other people out that she could see. No sounds, not even birds, and the sky overhead was a dull overcast grey. This whole town was lifeless, colorless, like a paint-by-numbers that hadn't been started yet.

Bree moved cautiously to the porch, glimpses of what she saw last night playing in her mind. Had she exaggerated it? Did she really see what she thought?

She rounded the edge of the porch and could see that the door was open. She froze. She'd seen enough to know she was right about last night. But she wanted to see more.

Bree's foot bent the bottom board on the steps, and it creaked. She moved slow, like it made her invisible. There was nothing inside the door. She took the next step, and she stood on the flat porch planks. She'd never been to this house in the six years since the guy moved in. Didn't even know his last name.

There was a blood stain on the floor just inside. It had been smeared and wiped in a swoosh like the Nike logo. She realized she never came to check on the guy last night. Maybe he was alive and suffering, and she ignored it because she didn't want to get involved.

"Hello?"

She stuck her head through the open door, not touching anything. "Hello?" she called again.

She moved one foot inside, careful to avoid the blood that had spread almost to the threshold. Bree saw the body near a tattered sofa. He was on his belly, one arm reaching out ahead of him. It looked like he had crawled there and smeared the blood under him as he went. She could see a cell phone on the small side table next to the sofa. His arm pointed to it like the arrow of a weather vane.

Bree watched his back for a long beat. No breathing. He might not have been dead right away, but he was dead now.

She backed out of the house and ran to her Civic. She had a moment of panic. Did she need to go clean up anything? Did her shoes leave imprints? If one of her hairs had fallen out, she'd be easy to identify. Did he have security cameras?

She calmed herself, rubbed her palms on her jeans to get rid of some phantom residue from being in the same room as a dead guy. Her first corpse outside of a funeral home.

Whatever trouble those two men had with each other, it was over now.

The old one took care of that. Bree knew at least one person she wished she had the courage to do that to—C-Money, the asshole feeding Katy his amateur meth samples trying to get her hooked and get her to sleep with him for a rock.

Chris had a gun, she knew that, but even if she wanted to lift it, she didn't know where he kept it. And she couldn't fool even herself into thinking she had the guts to kill someone, no matter how much she hated him. C-Money. Asshole. If anyone she ever met needed killing…

Chester tilted his head at the strange sounds coming from the old man. Carter kept trying to find the right fingering for *You've Got A Friend* but didn't have it yet. The old guitar sounded warm and felt smooth as a river stone in his hands. He wished he could coax the sounds out of it he knew it was meant to make. He gave up on James Taylor and plucked out a little twelve-bar blues, his fingers finding the familiar notes he'd tapped out a thousand times before. His hands knew where to go, even after years of the muscle memory laying dormant.

He'd picked up the guitar as a way to distract himself from thinking. He'd spent the morning wondering if he was really going to do something about Eddie. He decided no, it wasn't his place to make that call. He could scare him, intimidate him for Ivana—but killing was a whole different deal. And he knew now the way killing got into your bones, froze the marrow there, and made you harder.

"After all, I'm a killer," he said to Chester. "But who the hell am I fooling? I ain't Batman. Can't put on a mask and fix all the world's problems, even the assholes."

He didn't think it would be possible to get comfortable with the idea he was a killer, or someone who had killed at least. But it had already burrowed into his muscles as deep as those blues notes. Once you did something, that's who you were from there on out.

It's why he never stopped being a father, even after Audrey was dead and buried.

"It all adds up to a life, Chester." He scratched the old boy behind the ears

65

and got a grumble of approval. "Wonder what stories you could tell."

The gray in the dog's muzzle held a history, but it would forever be a secret to Carter. Best that way. Secrets are for keeping. They're about the only thing you can take with you to your grave.

He wondered if he should offer something to Ivana. Give her a way out. But he kept picking strings, making music. He didn't want his last few months to be spent plotting murders. One was enough, and it was behind him now. Stuffed in his back pocket, ready to be taken with him six feet under.

Bree met Halley Reid when she filed for emancipation eighteen months ago. Request denied. Halley had been the only one in the entire courthouse, or any government building, to show her an ounce of kindness or empathy. Twice her age, Halley had seen her own daughters in Bree, and told her so. And as her only black friend, Halley flew in the face of all the things Mama said about her race either out loud or muttered under her breath.

Halley sat behind a desk all day, facilitating and observing. She knew a little bit about every case brought into the small brick building. Theirs was a quiet county, mostly, and Halley had plenty of time to keep up on all the comings and goings. She often seemed to know more about the cases than the court-appointed lawyers.

She stood when Bree came around the corner to her desk.

"Hey, girl. Those sneakers sure were doing their job, sneaking up on me. Usually, I can hear everyone coming on these marble floors the second they come in the door."

She gave Bree a tight hug, and Bree loved every back-cracking second of it. Halley gave the longest hugs because, she told Bree once, "Whenever I see a kid come through here, I know they don't want to be in a courthouse. Only bad brought them here. So I know they're going through something, even if I don't know exactly what. And when you meet someone like that, you hang on until they let go because you don't know how much they need."

"Hey there," Bree said.

"What brings you here? Another petition?"

"No. I turned eighteen six months ago. No need anymore."

"Oh my goodness, that's right. So you're a free woman."

Bree choked on a laugh. "I'm about five grand away from free. But soon. I got a lot saved up. I'm outta here before long."

"Girl, you're gonna smash it, whatever you do. So you just here to say hi?"

"I had a favor."

Halley sat down again. "Don't they all?"

"Can you find an address for me from a license plate?"

Halley gave her a squint-eyed stare. "What for?"

Bree gave her the practiced lie. "There was a guy came around a few days ago looking for work. He wanted to mow our lawn. Mama sent him away, but now she changed her mind and wants to hire him. I only got the plates off his truck, not his name or phone number."

Halley looked at her skeptically. "You make a habit of writing down people's license numbers?"

"No. Just have a good memory for it, I guess. Seemed like a nice old guy, had a red truck. I remember things like that."

Halley tapped a pencil against her long nails. "That's a private citizen's information. Not really within the rules for me to give that out."

"All I want is to give the guy a job. He looked hard up, like he could use it."

"Girl, don't we all these days?" Halley laughed and shook her head at the sad truth of it. She faced her keyboard. "What's the number?"

Bree read it to her from memory. Halley tapped on the keys and waited. "Carter McCoy," she said and gave her an address way out of town.

"Thanks, Halley."

"For what?" she said, tapping the backspace button on her keyboard. "I didn't do anything." She raised both eyebrows at Bree, making sure she was understood. Bree nodded.

"Right." She took a pencil out of a cup on Halley's desk and a bright yellow Post-It note from a pile and wrote the address down.

"Thought you could remember stuff real good?"

Bree rode the lie further. "I see pictures. Like the truck and the plate. If I just hear it, I need to write it down."

"Mmm-hmm."

"Thanks a lot. I'll see you soon."

"Invitation still stands for dinner one night. You're an adult now; you don't need permission from your Mama."

"I will, I promise. One night when I'm not working."

"Hell, my kids would love it if you brought over some of them burgers. They love that greasy joint."

"Oh, I will, for sure. Thanks."

Bree walked away, her feet silent on the marble floors.

Carter rarely felt his age, but now he damn well did. Exhausted, but not from the weight of what he'd done. It came from losing the load he'd been carrying since the day Audrey died. He'd learned to haul it around with him without complaint, and now that it was gone, a tiredness came over him.

"Wish I could sleep as good as you," he said to Chester. The dog rolled over on his back, belly up, as if to show Carter how easy it was to just relax and take it easy.

Before he could lie down on the couch next to Chester, he heard a sound rarely heard out this way—a car approaching. The car was noisy and rattled on the rutted dirt drive. He went to the window and pulled back the shade, expecting police. What he saw was an old hatchback bouncing along, spitting dirt up behind it. The car slowed and came to a shuddering stop, then a girl in black jeans and a grey beanie on her head got out. She looked at the farmhouse like she'd been given bad information, which she probably had. Carter waited for her to turn around, but she didn't.

She knocked on the door and Chester lifted his head, ears up, and thumped his tail a few times.

"Easy, boy. Girl's probably lost or something."

He opened the door, and the girl took a step back. Something familiar about her, but he couldn't place it.

"Carter McCoy?"

He gave her a good long stare before saying, "Yeah."

"Can I come in and talk?"

"Depends. Who the hell are you?"

"My name's Breanna. You can call me Bree. I need to talk to you about something."

He didn't move to open the door any more than it was. "You selling something? 'Cause I ain't interested."

"I'm not a Girl Scout if that's what you mean. I do have a proposition for you, though."

"Spit it out then, girl. You don't need to come inside to tell me what you want from me. Time's short for some of us, you know."

She had a straight spine, clear eyes, pale skin. Something about her... Carter wanted her to keep talking. She drew him in. He thought he might just buy what she was selling. Confident girl, knew what she wanted. Good quality in a salesman.

The girl slipped the beanie off her head, exposing her red hair. "I saw you the other night."

It hit him like a brick dropped off a roof. She was the girl next door.

Carter wanted to sit down. He wanted that nap. He wanted to be anywhere but in this conversation, even as much as he wanted her to keep talking only a second ago.

"What do you mean?"

"Let's not do that," she said. "I saw you shoot that guy."

He looked to her car. No police behind her. No sires in the distance. She hadn't screamed that night. Maybe she wasn't there to bust him.

"Okay. Come out with it. Is that all you came here to tell me?"

"No. I came to ask you if you'd do it again. For me. As a favor."

Her confidence had slipped. He guessed she had practiced the words in a mirror or something, but spitting them out for real had made her wobble a bit. Maybe they both could use a sit-down.

Carter stepped back from the door and pulled it wide. "C'mon in."

He got them both Cokes, and she sat next to Chester on the couch. The old hound sat up and slapped his tail against the cushions until they kicked up dust. She had longer, sharper nails than Carter, better for scratching.

Carter handed her the glass bottle of Coke.

"What's his name?" she asked.

"Chester."

"He's a sweet boy."

"He farts."

"Yeah, like you don't." She gave him a firm pat on the head. "You're a good boy, aren't you?"

Carter sat in the armchair across from her. "You mind telling me what you meant, but what you said out there? Do it again?"

She took a quick swig of Coke and set the bottle down on the coffee table. "Okay, look, I know a guy who's way worse than the guy you shot. I need him gone and out of my life so I can get out of this town and have a real chance in life."

"Someone keeping you from leaving?"

"My friend. Katy. We're leaving together, once we save up a bit. But he's bad. A drug dealer. He's got her using and spending our stash."

"You want me to kill a drug dealer."

He said it flat, business-like.

"Yeah." She picked up the Coke and took a deeper swig. He could see her have a hard time swallowing. She put on a good face, but she was nervous. Carter felt a twinge in his gut, like his illness wanted to remind him it was still there. The stress of this unwanted conversation woke the monster living inside him.

"Why don't you call the cops for that? Seems like their business."

"He doesn't need to get thrown in a cell for a weekend and then get out. If he did and he knew I called the police, he'd kill me."

"So don't tell him it was you."

"He'd know."

"How?"

"He would, okay?"

Her frustration showed. Maybe the sudden sugar and caffeine rush was grinding on her edges.

"Okay, so he would. What's it got to do with me?"

"It's…what you do."

Carter shook his head. "No, it ain't. That was a one-time thing."

"What was so special about that guy?"

"That's between me and him."

He turned away from her, clenched his teeth until his jaw was sore. Bree stood, wandered the edges of the room, looking at picture frames, his wall of books, the unfinished jigsaw puzzle.

"I saw you. You haven't denied it."

"Okay, so you have eyes."

"Got a mouth too. Could use it. Go to the cops, like you say."

Carter got her implication. She was young, but didn't act it.

"Tell on me, huh? That it?"

"I could."

A pain gripped his stomach. Carbonation wasn't good for him anymore. Whatever kind of battery acid they put in the secret formula to Coca-Cola, either. He tried to keep it hidden from the girl. Carter bent forward and set his bottle down, then kept his body bent. He bit down on the grunt of pain in his throat.

"Unless you do this for me," she said. The bargain had been laid out, but she kept her back to him. Brave enough to say the words, but not enough to look at him while she did.

Carter didn't answer. Anything he tried to grit out now would sound like a strangled horse. His silence unnerved the girl.

"I don't want to tell," she said. "I don't know that guy next door. He probably deserved it. Most men do. I don't want to rat on you, but I will."

The pain faded, leaving a sheen of sweat across his forehead. He sat back in the chair.

"Unless I kill this guy?"

"Just the same way. Do it the same."

"I told you I'm not a killer."

"Not from what I saw."

She had him there.

Bree sat back down. She picked up the bottle in one hand and took a drink, scratched Chester with the other.

"You're trying to push me into a corner."

"I don't have many other ideas," she said.

"So you can leave town?"

"Leave this town, leave my house, leave my Mama. You don't know what it's like to be stuck like your feet are in cement. I look out every night when the sun goes down, and I think about all the places over there. All the people and the opportunities. All I want is a chance to chase that sun."

He knew now what the bright eyes and straight spine reminded him of. It wasn't so much the girl on the porch that night—it was Audrey.

"Why not do it yourself?"

"Oh, Jesus, I couldn't."

Carter nodded to himself. That's what I thought.

"Plus, I'd get caught."

"And I won't?"

"I don't see any cops here now, do you?"

She had him again.

He took another sip of Coke. "Tell me more about this man."

Carter ended up convincing himself more than Bree convinced him to do it. There was a brick wall between this girl and her future, and he'd seen one girl miss out on a future already. Why else was he still here but to make things right? He'd given Justin what he deserved, and now he could give someone else a chance at making a life Audrey missed out on.

This guy, Cash Money, sounded like a real piece of work, too. Pushing drugs on young kids, trading highs for sex from underage girls. What was this jerk contributing to society?

It was a slippery slope, he knew, becoming judge and jury and executioner. It was usually saved for the comic pages. But he could do some real good here. And who would miss a guy like that with a goofy name?

He gave her another Coke. "So what are you gonna do when you get out of here?"

"I don't know exactly." She scratched Chester behind the ear. "Something with animals would be nice. I'm sort of at a one-step-at-a-time stage right now. As long as I can stop working at Burger Barn and running errands for Mama, then I'll consider it a huge step up, career-wise."

"It's good to have a plan," he said. "Even a vague one."

"Okay, you're right. I'll work on it."

"So where's your dad?"

"Ran off. If you knew Mama, you wouldn't wonder why."

"Ah. I see."

"Yeah."

"So if I'm gonna do this," Carter said. "There needs to be no connection

75

between us. We can't talk on the phone or meet in public."

"I get it. I don't want to get caught."

"Neither do I, but it'd be worse for you."

"It's not really hiring a hitman if I don't pay you, is it?"

"I'm no hitman."

"Well…"

He nearly raised his voice to her, wanted to let her know how wrong she was. He was doing a good thing. Killing Justin was a good thing. A necessary thing.

"You didn't exactly give me a choice here."

"I know. I'm sorry. I didn't know where else to go."

"I guess it's good you don't know a lot of people you could call when you want to kill a drug dealer. Says something about you."

Bree nearly choked on her Coke, the bubbles rushing back up her throat.

"Yeah. Something."

She watched him as he stared off into nothing, in thought again. He seemed to do that, the old man. Still, she liked him. He had a kind quality, like she always wanted from a Grandpa. All she got was a grumpy old fart who died when she was six and never once gave her a birthday or Christmas present. Any guy who could have a dog like the lazy beast on the couch couldn't be all bad. Even if he did kill people.

There was more here to him, this Carter McCoy. A much larger story. But Bree wasn't telling her tale, and she decided his might be best kept to himself as well.

"So, I don't see you or talk to you again, I guess?"

"Unless I need more to go on, but you told me where he usually works and what he looks like, so...you shouldn't need to come back."

"All right." Bree stood. "Nice doing business with you."

"I don't want you thinking this is nice business at all, young lady. This is taking a man's life. Nothing nice about it. It's just a question if he's *less* nice."

"Well, he is, trust me."

"I'll take your word. Wish I could get your word that you'll stick to our agreement and leave my name out of the other business with your neighbor."

"You can trust me, Carter."

She held out her hand, and he looked at it. He took her pale hand in his. She felt his callouses and the bones poking through the thin skin.

"You make something of this, Bree," Carter said, looking her in the eye in such a way it unnerved her. "You get an open stretch of road, and you run for the horizon and don't look back, okay?"

"Once I'm out of here, I ain't never coming back."

"It's not just that." He kept a tight grip on her hand. "Make something of your new life. Do things. Make your own way. Appreciate that not everyone had the opportunity to do what you get a chance to do."

"I will."

Bree almost leaned in and hugged him. This man could teach her things. This man learned by living, and that's just what she intended to do. As soon as that roadblock was out of the way.

The flashing lights made Bree think of Christmas even though summer hadn't officially started yet. Four police cars strobed the usually quiet street. The lone ambulance almost made Bree laugh. Neighbors she hadn't seen in months stood out on their front porches to get a look at the moment when they wheeled the black body bag out of the neighbor's front door.

She worried that they were inside gathering evidence to catch Carter. That he'd end up in jail for this murder before he could complete the one she wanted. But this wasn't a big city with a crime lab and all that TV show science. Unless Carter had been careless, he'd be okay. Then again, he'd let her witness the whole thing, so how diligent had he been with the rest of it?

Bree made her way quickly inside her house.

"Shit, girl, where've you been? There's a goddamn murder next door." Despite the lure of the crime scene outside, Mama was still in her chair. Bree couldn't be sure if she'd gotten up at some point earlier and gone outside or if some neighbor had filled her in on the action through the screen door.

"Serious?" she said.

"Yeah. That creep who lived next door got himself shot. You get my dip?"

Bree tossed the plastic bag over to Mama, who dug in it and came out with her tin of Skoal.

"So what happened over there?"

"I don't know, except a guy got killed."

"Guess we should lock the doors."

"Nah, I bet it was someone he knew who wanted him dead. Don't have nothing to do with us."

"Still, a killer's running around."

"Breanna, there's a million killers running around. They say you pass at least six serial killers on the street over your life."

Fewer for Mama, thought Bree. *Since she never leaves the house.*

"Chris home?"

"Nah, he's out," Mama said with a wave of her hand like she was swatting away a moth. Her attention was back on the TV, watching a true crime show this time. Inspired by real life next door, Bree assumed. Game shows didn't hold her attention when death lay only one weedy yard away.

There was never a need to end a conversation with Mama. No need to excuse herself to her bedroom. As soon as Bree's usefulness was wrung out like a damp rag—picking up things from the store, cashing her weekly check from Burger Barn—the conversation was over, and the world inside the TV set held more allure than her own child ever could. Bree left her Mama and the TV blaring, the lights pulsing through the windows like there was a dance club on the front lawn.

Bree locked her bedroom door, but not because of the killing. She'd met that murderer, and he was a surprisingly nice guy. She made a habit of locking herself in and locking Chris and Mama out.

She called Katy.

"How are you?"

"Fine. Better," Katy said. "Hey, I'm really sorry about yesterday. I just…I get weak, you know?"

"It's okay. We just have to keep our eyes on the prize, y'know? If we stick to the plan, we'll be in California by the end of summer."

"Jesus, that'd be nice to not have to spend another winter here."

"I know." She wanted to tell Katy about the murder next door and what she knew about it that the cops didn't, but she kept it to herself. Katy hadn't proved herself entirely reliable. And since Bree had just enlisted the old man to kill C-Money and take Katy's supply away, she didn't want her to run off and tell the bastard in a fit of craving.

"I promise I won't fuck up again," Katy said.

"I know. Our problems are gonna be over soon, I swear."

"I think he's getting suspicious."

Katy's dad, no need to name him. Bree knew.

"Why do you say that?"

"Just a feeling."

He probably could tell that she'd been getting high. They never knew how obvious it is to the rest of the world, and the way he hovered around her room, always peeking in, opening doors without knocking, "accidentally" catching her changing, that bastard would know if his little girl was using. That would bring down a beating. If he knew she was saving up to ditch this town, he'd smash that piggy bank and take the money for himself.

"We just need to keep on going like normal for a few more months. Show up at our jobs and put the money away."

"Sometimes he gives me this look like he knows everything, and I feel like the volcano is gonna erupt, y'know?"

"Just avoid him. That's what I do with Chris."

"Yeah, yeah."

"You be good."

"Yeah, you too."

"Katy...I'm serious."

"I know. Me too. I will, I swear."

They clicked off, and Bree laid back in bed and thought about California and all the things they had there that weren't in Minnesota. Seagulls, movie stars, earthquakes. Any of it was better than blizzards of snow in winter and swarms of mosquitos in summer. Any life was better than this one.

Homicide detective Brian DeFore sometimes resented the stenciled job title on his door. He hadn't investigated a homicide in over two years. He spent his time helping out the burglary division, digging into cold cases from before his time, all of which remained cold since the guy before him was such a lazy dumbass whose record-keeping skills were subpar at best.

When the chief of police came through his door without knocking, he knew something different had happened. Chief Winters only came this far down the hall on special occasions, and there hadn't been one of those since Ed LeFarge had dug up bones on his property that turned out to be those of his own great-grandfather who'd been buried on the property and hadn't been moved when the headstone was relocated back in 1948.

"Brian, you caught one." The chief slapped a thin manila folder down on DeFore's desk.

Chief Winters smiled like he was talking about catching a particularly big fish on a weekend boat trip, not a dead body turning up in his jurisdiction for the first time in years.

"An actual H word?"

"Homicide with a capital H."

DeFore tried not to reach for it like he was excited. Someone had died, after all. But he opened the folder and read with interest.

"Male, caucasian…bullet wound…no forced entry…"

DeFore spoke with an upper-Midwest accent, so thick people often thought he was joking. He was raised on the Upper Peninsula and had only ever traveled as far south as Chicago in his whole life. For six years, he

82

ran the homicide division for the entire county and, in six years, had never been busy once.

"Have at it, DeFore. If you still remember how."

DeFore had to look up from the report to make sure Chief Winters was kidding. Indeed, there was a smile on his face. He looked at his one and only homicide detective like a coach proud of a kid who broke a slump with a winning home run.

"I'll get on it right away, Chief."

"Damn right, you will. And if you need help, I've got Nava set aside for you."

"I've got it for now, even if I am a little rusty." He forced a smile, getting in on the joke.

"Go get 'em." Chief Winters gave him a thumbs up and, if DeFore was right, a little wink.

Brian DeFore stopped wearing the department-mandated jacket and tie years ago, and nobody cared. He wore a light blue chambray shirt and jeans. Helped him interview people, he said. Less intimidating. He kept fit, wore his hair short, and his face shaved. Nothing about him said cop, which also helped him interview, though homicides were so rare around here he didn't get much chance to use his skills. There aren't many people in the world who wish more citizens got killed closer to home, but DeFore was one of them.

DeFore arrived at the crime scene and got out of his unmarked car. *Like riding a bike*, he thought. It was all coming back to him.

He walked the scene, spoke to the officer on duty, wrote in a notebook, paged through the coroner's photos. He wished they'd called him in sooner, but few of the officers working in town had ever been on a homicide at all. Nobody was up on exact procedures. But this was DeFore's investigation now. And he had a killer to catch.

Carter led Chester through the rows of headstones. Chester sniffed each grave like he was trying to read the names etched in the marble by braille. Carter stopped over Ava and Audrey's plot. Birds flitted and chirped, chasing each other and landing on the stones for a second before dashing off to another, filled with spring energy and hope. Tiny shoots of new grass sprouted up from the dark dirt of a fresh grave.

"So I did the thing," Carter said to Audrey's grey stone. "It's all over. I don't know if you rested any easier last night, but it's done. I know he's not in the same place as you. But he's dead, same as you, finally."

He studied the numbers of her born and died dates.

"I still can't tell if it was the right thing to do, but I guess it doesn't matter now."

He turned to Ava. "I'm sorry if you disapprove. Guess that doesn't much matter either. Just know I didn't do it when I wanted to because I knew you didn't approve. I waited a long damn time so I wouldn't have to see you give me that look you get when I've let you down. I could deal with years of letting myself down, thinking I wasn't doing the right thing as a father and a man, if it meant not letting you down."

Chester lay down in the grass.

"I won't even get into what comes next. Seems I walked into it this time. I got seen, and now she wants me to do another thing, and I don't have much choice if I want to stay out of jail."

Carter chuckled to himself.

"Y'know, Audrey, I think you'd like her, this girl. Got red hair like you

84

always wanted. Doesn't suffer fools. I might be keeping my old ass out of the slammer, but I think I might help her too. I guess we'll see, won't we?"

Carter turned to walk away but stopped. He looked down at Chester snoozing on his side, then up to the blank space on the gravestone next to Ava. Carter laid down, his head near the stone and his feet stretched out. Beside him, Chester let out a deep sigh. Carter lay there watching the birds swoop by overhead. They moved like they had important places to be, but ended up back on the same stone where they started. Little brown birds that would fit in your palm, necks twitching and chirps sounding at once musical and frightened.

"Excuse me, sir?"

Carter looked up to see a man in overalls with the name "Al" stitched over the breast. "Can I help you?"

"No." Carter didn't move.

Al looked left and then right. "You can't sleep here."

"Not sleeping," Carter said as he closed his eyes and felt the sun burn orange through his eyelids. "Just trying it on for size."

Carter liked to sit out back and listen to the night sounds. He loved watching the bats fly at dusk and then catch a glimpse of a pair of shining eyes on the edges of the trees. All the creatures who hid during the day and then spent their waking hours clinging to the darkness. A life hidden away.

He'd never considered himself someone with secrets. Now he had a big one, and keeping it covered depended on this girl with the red hair.

Chester perked up at a sound off in the darkness.

"This girl deserves a chance, right?" he asked. "Hell, boy, maybe we are like Batman."

Chester barked once.

"Yeah, you're right. Batman never kills anyone. Maybe we're more like The Punisher."

Chester lay his head back down. Carter checked his watch.

"Well, let's head out. You're supposed to be a hunting dog. Let's go hunt."

Bree had given him the name of a park where she said he could find C-Money working once the sun went down. A regular fox in the henhouse, this guy. Living in the shadows for protection.

Carter parked the truck away from any street lights and waited. Chester took up most of the bench seat, his long legs dangling off the edge, but when sleep took him, nothing would keep his eyes open.

Carter sipped on a Coke in a glass bottle. There was little movement in the park save for the swarms of moths around the tall light stanchions.

"Guess this is what we do now. Stakeouts." Chester stayed asleep.

After a half hour of nothing, two figures moved into the park and sat down on a small merry-go-round. They didn't spin it, only sat, and in a minute, Carter saw plumes of cigarette smoke over their heads. The way a spider appears from nowhere once a fly is caught in his web, a third figure appeared from the shadows. The new man was tall and thin. He walked to them with purpose. They traded greetings, and a transaction went down. The two figures moved away quickly once their business was done, and they walked past where Carter was parked. He stayed perfectly still and hoped Chester wouldn't rouse when he heard them walk past, but he didn't. As they went by, Carter could see they were only teenagers. Their faces held none of the anxious energy of youth. They were both desperate rats seeking shelter again away from prying eyes.

He saw what Bree meant about this man preying on kids.

He watched as the tall man faded back into the shadows. Carter started the truck and drove slowly along the side of the park where he'd seen the man walk. At the very edge, under a tall tree, was a two-door sports car parked with no lights on.

Carter eased the truck by in idle. He let his lights pass over the car and then chase the shadows away as he came up from behind. He got even with the car and stopped. He could see the back of C-Money's head in the driver's seat.

He'd brought the gun. Before he left home, he loaded one bullet and brought six more with him. The rifle was still in the case on the floor in front of Chester. Unless another customer came into the park, they were alone. No witnesses this time.

Cash Money turned around and put his hand up to block the light and try to get a look into Carter's cab.

"The fuck you want?"

Carter leaned over and unzipped the gun case.

"Yo, I don't do business here. Go wait at the merry-go-round 'til I'm finished, yo."

Carter had the rifle halfway out when another face appeared, eyes catching the headlight glare through the window. The girl lifted up from C-Money's lap. Her eyes showed fear, thinking cops or worse—her parents.

"Hey, don't stop. I tell you to stop?" He turned back to Carter, shouting to be heard from inside the car. "I said get the fuck out of here. Get your shit somewhere else." He forced the girl's head back into his lap.

Carter pushed the gun back inside the case and hit the gas. He didn't need another witness and didn't want some innocent girl getting blood on her. She was already in a bad enough place if she was here after midnight in a car with a drug dealer.

Carter drove two blocks and pulled over. He turned the truck to face the direction of the park. If C-Money drove straight when his night was over, Carter could follow him. Otherwise, he'd have to wait to complete his deal with Bree.

Bree lay on her back, unable to fall asleep. Mama had the TV blaring even though she'd fallen asleep in her chair hours ago. Chris wasn't home yet. He rarely was before dawn. Bree's same twin bed she'd had since she was nine didn't cut it anymore. Just like this town, it was too small, filthy with too many stains of the past, and she'd outgrown the style.

She hadn't eaten dinner, and her stomach growled at her, though she knew she couldn't eat, and the turmoil in her gut was mostly from what she'd asked the old man to do. What she'd *forced* him to do.

She hadn't liked blackmailing him like that, but she had no choice. Maybe if she hadn't liked him so much. He wasn't at all what she'd expected of a killer. She knew he had to have some sort of heart since he hadn't turned the gun on her the night she saw him, but any man with a sweet old dog like that had to have a good heart, right?

Bree had noticed the photos around his place of him with a woman she guessed was his wife. Beyond those, there was no indication of a woman living there. Nothing folded, pillows off-kilter, no cooking smells. She didn't want to fit the old lady into a stereotype, but women of that age were always the ones with a full candy dish and an air freshener plugged into a wall socket. His house had none of that.

A thin strip of moonlight cut through the window and lit the floor like a rope had been laid across. She gave up on sleeping and sat up, pissed off at her racing mind because she'd drawn the dreaded breakfast shift tomorrow. The great hungover and the nightshift workers getting off collided in an amphetamine comedown haze to mumble orders for hash-browns and reheated egg sandwiches before stumbling off to bed like vampires racing the sunrise. In the closet, behind a plastic set of drawers with hair ties, her hairdryer, face creams, and all the other stuff she didn't want to leave in the bathroom for Chris to either use, throw out, or otherwise mess with, was a small fire safe. She'd bought it at a Walmart a year ago, and even though it would barely hold a footlong Subway sandwich, she promised that when it was filled with cash, she and Katy were out of there.

She thumbed through her savings as if she didn't know down to the dollar how much was there. What she didn't know was how much Katy had blown in her dabbles in meth and heroin, and who knew what else. The bills in her hand might have to be enough to get to the coast, and if so, then so be it. She was gonna get there if she had to hitchhike in winter.

Chester's bark woke Carter with a jerk, his knee hitting the bottom of the steering wheel. He worried for a second he'd fallen asleep while driving, but he'd really dozed off fours before on his stakeout. The sun hadn't crested the horizon yet but offered a grey glow to the world as if it was politely trying to ease everyone from sleep slowly, not the way Chester had just done to Carter.

The car was gone, the park empty.

"Well, shit."

Chester barked again.

"Okay, buddy, I hear you."

Carter ran his fingers through his thin white hair and went to the passenger door to ease Chester down. He walked him around the edge of the park, and Chester peed three times, each one reminding Carter that he also had to go fiercely. He walked to the far corner of the park, to the edge of a line of trees, checked over his shoulder, and then unzipped his pants.

"You keep lookout," he said to Chester.

When he was done and turned around, someone had entered the park. A teenage boy, or early twenties. He moved erratically, pacing in front of the merry-go-round, his hand pressed a cell phone to his ear. Hopefully not calling the cops on Carter's public urination, but from the looks of it, the kid was oblivious to the world around him.

Carter stuck to the tree line, moving slowly back toward the truck. Chester sniffed the trails of every squirrel who passed through here for the last week.

The car returned. C-Money. The kid pulled the phone away from his ear and flung his hands up in the air as if to say, "Where've you been?"

Carter froze with Chester taut on the end of his leash, hoping he wouldn't bark.

The kid came to the open window of C-Money's car. An exchange was made, but before the kid could get more than a step away, Carter heard C-Money call after the kid, "Next time, call me during normal business hours, right? This was a favor for you. Just lucky I was still up."

The kid ignored him and quick-stepped out of the park. The car roared away from the curb, and Carter took off in a run. Chester did his best to keep up on his old hips. By the time they got back to the truck, they were both panting for air. He caught up to the car three blocks away after rolling through two stop signs. He saw the car turn right up ahead, and he slowed his pace and fell in behind him.

Carter stole a glance at the gun case on the floor next to him. The zipper wasn't fully closed from last night, and he could see the barrel poking out. His heart raced, and his gut suddenly seized with a contraction. Any kind of stress these days sent him into a spell. He knew it would pass and grit his teeth to the pain. He let out a grunt from deep inside, and Chester gave him a sidelong look. The dog was awake, watching out the window, feeling the electricity in the cab and Carter's nervous energy.

Carter focused on the car and not so much on the streets or where they were going. It wasn't until he turned onto the street that he realized where they were. Crime scene tape still criss-crossed the doorway of Justin's house. Carter swore he could still hear the echo of the gunshot.

C-Money parked his car in front of the house next door. The screen door opened, and the red-haired girl stepped out, clipping on a name tag to the chest of a brown and mustard yellow uniform of that Burger Barn place.

C-Money smiled at her as she walked past him on the walkway. He sang a few bars of "9 to 5" and she told him, "Fuck off, Chris."

"Hey, we're both workin' for that paper. I just have different hours than you."

She ignored him and got behind the wheel of the crap Honda she'd driven to Carter's house. He didn't stop to ask questions, just gunned the engine and drove away.

Back home, Carter tipped two white pills into his palm. He'd avoided the painkillers from his doctor until now. They were "just to take the edge off," according to the doc, but he needed the drugs to calm his nerves and slow his heartbeat.

He let Chester out back and sat with a cup of warmed-over coffee from yesterday and watched the dog follow scent trails up and down the lawn in the dawn light.

The redhead, Bree, knew this Cash Money guy. Lived with him, it looked like. This was more than he expected, and somehow being caught off guard had made it seem more real and sordid than he'd convinced himself it was. For a brief moment, he could see it from the outside, and he realized he was about to kill a man just because someone asked him to.

He breathed deep and let the pills work their way into his system. The coffee probably wouldn't help his nerves, but he needed the morning ritual.

Chester lifted his leg and then trotted back to the porch, looking at Carter expectantly. Carter checked his watch and the dog was right: time for his breakfast. He stood and busied himself with the task, grateful for something to take his mind off things.

The pills were fogging his mind by the time Chester was done eating. Carter sat on the couch and felt a gentle kind of paralysis come over his muscles. He felt relaxed and untroubled. He could only wonder if this was the feeling those kids in the park were chasing with the junk they bought from C-Money. He saw the appeal.

Chester came and sat beside him, laying his head on Carter's lap, his jowls still wet from his meal, but Carter didn't care.

Bree's shift dragged on, like they all did. The morning was moderately busy. Nothing the small crew of four couldn't handle. Three were other teenagers like Bree, and then there was Neil, the shift manager. Bree often wondered if Neil had some sort of special need. Good for him for locking down a managerial job if he did; a damn shame for him if he didn't.

She wondered if when she got to California, the ocean breezes could waft away the smell of fry grease from her hair and her pores. First thing she'd do is bathe in the ocean and get rid of all the smells of this town.

The menu had switched from breakfast to lunch, and the sizzle of frozen beef patties being made edible again filled her ears like she was standing next to a wasp's nest. The piped-in music was all songs that sounded vaguely familiar and yet somehow off, like corporate had chosen cover versions of popular songs performed by bands who didn't speak English as their primary language.

The customers didn't care. Just hand over the twelve hundred calories of grease and cheese, and let's pretend none of this ever happened.

A mom came in with two grotesquely obese children. Looking at them made Bree sad, but then so did most of the people around here.

Time was measured in orders completed. She tapped the register with the photos of items rather than words in case she was too stupid to read. She took cash now and then, but mostly people used cards, and when she offered to upgrade them from a medium to a large for only fifty cents more, they usually took her up on it, which always surprised her because she knew her sales job was terrible. She said the words flat and devoid of meaning, but the Burger Barn customers only heard "more," and they bleated like sheep and fell in line.

She clocked out at three without saying goodbye to anyone and went to get lunch somewhere else.

She wanted to go home and sleep, but she also didn't want to go to *her* home. So she drove to Katy's. She parked her Civic out front and stiffened when she saw a familiar car parked a little further along the street.

Bree moved quickly around the side of the house to Katy's window. She crept up close and put a foot on the spigot, raising herself until she could see inside.

Chris was there, sitting on Katy's bed. She was holding a glass pipe to her lips, trying to get an empty Bic lighter to fire while he rubbed his hand on her thigh.

Why the fuck was he still alive? Bree thought.

Katy got a small spark and then a flame and set it to the bulb, drawing in deep like a thirsty woman finding water in the desert. Chris kept rubbing his hand higher up on her thigh. A white cloud hovered over them.

She pulled the pipe away, and Chris went in for a kiss. Katy brushed a sloppy hand, still holding the lighter, in front of her like Chris was a mosquito trying to drain her blood, which wasn't very far from true.

"Knock it off."

"Hey, come on now." His voice was soothing, smooth. "I told you I wouldn't charge cash, but it ain't free."

He went in for another kiss. The smoke had energized her, and she pointed her dilated eyes at him like laser beams. "Then I'll pay cash."

God dammit, Bree thought. *Our money.*

The honey was gone from Chris's voice. "Then why the fuck did you ask me to come in?"

"Not to fuck you."

"Then what? To get high? Well, I did my end of the bargain. I met your expectations. Time for you to meet mine." He moved his body on top of hers. Katy fought, never letting go of the pipe or the lighter.

It bothered Bree how calculated his argument was, like a cheap lawyer.

She couldn't wait to go back to the old man. She couldn't sit and watch this. Bree pushed open the window.

"Let her fucking go, Chris."

Chris jumped off her like he'd been electrocuted. He looked around the room for the invader, and when he settled on Bree coming in through the window, he relaxed.

"Jesus Christ, Bree. Get out of here. This doesn't concern you."

"You get out, Chris. Right fucking now."

Katy moved up the bed to her headboard, curling in on herself. Seeing Bree, tears came to her eyes.

"I said fucking get out, Bree."

"I'm not leaving, so unless you think you can get it up with me watching, then you better leave."

Chris stood up and threw a pillow to the floor. "God dammit."

"I know where her dad keeps all his guns, too, so start walking and keep on going, motherfucker."

"What is your fucking problem, Bree?"

"You're an asshole, that's what my problem is. And hers, too."

Bree climbed onto the bed and snatched the pipe from Katy's hand. She let it go easily. Bree threw the still-warm pipe at Chris. "And take this shit with you."

Chris slapped it away in the air and let it fall to the floor, where it shattered on the hardwood.

"You got a fuckin' attitude problem, Breanna," Chris said. "Those counselors were right."

"Just go."

"Fine. Whatever. Go lez out with your girlfriend. Fuck you both." He got to the door and turned, aiming a finger at Katy. "You owe me thirty bucks, bitch."

He left through the front door, which told Bree that Katy's dad wasn't home. None of this would happen under his roof while he was there.

Bree stood facing the bedroom door, fists clenched and breathing hard until she heard the front door slam and then heard Chris's car peel away from the curb outside. Only then did she turn to Katy, who was still curled on the bed like she was one of the tangled sheets.

Bree sat down gently on the edge of the bed. Katy wept.

"I'm so sorry. I'm so sorry, Bree."

Bree was still angry, but she set a hand on Katy's back and rubbed her.

"I don't know what…" Katy started, but she let the sobs take over.

"It's all right. I'm gonna take care of it. I promise."

Bree knew her next stop was back out to see the old man and find out what the hell happened and why the hell it *hadn't* happened.

Maybe banging a fist onto the door of a known killer wasn't the smartest idea, but so few of Bree's good ideas had worked out so far. The old man answered the door, looking like he just woke up from a nap.

"What the hell, McCoy?"

"I could ask you the same thing."

Bree leaned forward at the waist. "Why is he still alive?"

"Why was he at your house?"

She leaned back, her mouth gone slack. Carter stepped back and opened the door wide.

"Maybe you better come on in."

Bree walked past him, and the dog looked up briefly from the couch and then lay his head back down with a sigh. Bree tried to get the same fight back in her voice.

"I thought you were going to take care of things."

"I was until I saw you two pass by each other in your front yard, looking like you knew each other. Looking like you were roommates."

"He's my brother, okay?

A silence settled over them. Both were angry; both had questions.

"I'm out," Carter said.

"You can't be out. I'll go to the police."

"You know I can tell them you tried to hire me to kill your brother, right?"

"Who will they believe, the one who already killed a guy or the little girl next door? You'll spend the rest of your life in prison, man."

Carter puffed out a laugh. "You know, I don't think your little threats

99

mean as much as you think they do, girly."

"If you don't think I'll do it, you're wrong. I am so fed up with this place I'll burn the whole goddamn thing down before I let it drag me under."

"Oh, I know you'll do it. Just look at you. Your face is more red than your hair. I'm sure you have a good reason to want your brother out of your life. But you send me to jail for the rest of my life, you know how long that will be? Measure it in weeks, kid. 'Cause that's all I got left."

Carter wiped saliva off his stubbled chin that had slipped out when he raised his cracking voice. He stood still, looking at the floor, chest puffing in and out. Bree stared at him, not fully understanding yet.

"I know you're old, but…"

"Not just old. Dying. And I don't really give a shit what you do to me."

He sat down in a heap on the couch next to Chester, who didn't even look up.

Bree moved slowly to the armchair and sat.

"Shit. I'm sorry."

"What for? You were about to ruin my life anyway when you thought it would go on much longer."

She turned her head away like she'd been slapped. "You don't know what it's like to live with him. And to have him fuck up my plans."

"Yeah, well, plans rarely work out the way you want them to. Welcome to life, kid."

They sat for a while with only the sound of Chester's breathing.

"I just want to make something of myself, and I can't do that here. Not with my family."

"Family's about the only thing I ever cared about."

"You're lucky." They weren't looking at each other. The anger had dissipated like a candle had been snuffed, the smoke lingering but the fire gone. "My mom sucks. I never knew my dad. I just caught my brother trying to rape my best friend."

"What?"

"It's what he does, Carter. He takes from everyone he meets. He never gives anything. He blames me for Dad running off, but it was before I was even born."

"How the hell is that your fault then?"

"He stuck around until Chris was three. Then, when Mama found out she was pregnant, he bolted. Chris blames me. Doesn't have to make sense in his world."

Carter rubbed his palms together, staring into them, avoiding her eyes.

"That's rough. But I can't fix all that for you. Not with a bullet."

"Yeah, but a bullet or a knife can cut through the ropes, tying me down here. All I want is a chance."

Carter ran a hand over his skull, smoothing down his bedhead.

"I'm hungry. You hungry?"

Bree shifted in her chair, unsure. "I guess I could eat."

"You like Mexican food?"

Carter drove to Mesa Grande by habit, but when he turned the corner and saw the sign, he thought twice. He shouldn't be seen with Bree, especially not at a place he frequented. If he was going to do this, and her story had set him back on the path to helping her out, brother or not, then they needed to keep their lives separate.

He drove past the parking lot to Mesa Verde and went an extra half block to a fried chicken place.

"Y'know what, I changed my mind."

"Aw, no, I like that place."

"You know it?"

"Yeah, I eat there all the time. C'mon, this chicken is so greasy."

He pulled into the small lot and could see smoke curling from the roof of the chicken place. Even with the windows up, the fry oil in the air seeped through. Carter tapped his fingers on the steering wheel.

"Yeah, okay. But you stay here. We shouldn't be seen together."

"Won't people just think you're my grandpa?"

"It's not what they think now. It's what they remember later. And a white-haired old man walking around with a carrot-top teenager is memorable."

Bree blew air out her nose and folded her arms across her chest. "Fine. I guess you're right."

"I'll walk over. You know what you want? The enchiladas are good."

"I always get the fish tacos."

"Okay then." He pushed open his door.

"With rice and beans. Black beans."

102

He stood with the door open. "Anything else?"

"And get me a horchata. They make it homemade there."

"I know."

He shut the door and looked around for prying eyes as he walked back to the sidewalk. He listened to cicadas in the trees as he walked the rest of the block to Mesa Grande. Here, the air smelled of chili and spices, cilantro, and pork barbacoa on the grill. Muffled sounds of Mexican music lifted over the parking lot. Yeah, better than fried chicken.

Ivana gave him a smile when he walked in. It was a busy night. Three tables already, and Ivana there all alone to do the cooking and waitressing. Guess her daughter had better things to do.

She passed him carrying two plates of food still steaming from the kitchen. "The usual?"

"Yes, and fish tacos too."

Ivana set the plates down at a booth and came back, pushing a curl of hair from her sweat-slick forehead.

"That dog moving up from beef burritos?"

"No, it's for a friend." He worried it was a mistake to come here. "But now that you mention it, give me one of those burritos too. He'll be mad if I come home empty-handed."

"To go?"

"Yeah."

She didn't need to write it down. "You should bring your friend in sometime."

He heard the tone of her voice, the way the words curled at the edges. He knew what she was thinking. "It's not a ladyfriend, if that's what you mean. Just a kid who's mowing my lawn for me. I'm paying him shit, so I figure the least I could do is buy him lunch."

He ordered the two drinks, and Ivana went away to cook the food. The lie had worked.

He sat at the counter and listened to the music, the muted conversations. These people had no idea they were in the presence of a killer. One who leaned toward killing again. How many times had he sat somewhere and had a murderer nearby?

It struck him as odd that he really didn't feel that different. He knew something was off, but the growing whiskers on his chin felt more like a change than the fact that he had gone seventy-two years without being a killer, then in one pull of the trigger, he became one.

He had to feel down lower to find it, but there it was. It was a mark on him. Permanent, like a tattoo, but hidden away. Only those he chose to show it to would ever know.

Ivana brought out his bag of food, and he paid her. Two of the tables had gone. Only one couple left. When she brought him his change, she lowered her voice.

"I wanted to tell you, Carter. I'm going to do it. I'm going to kick Eddie out."

Carter couldn't help breaking into a wide grin. "Really? Good for you."

Ivana smiled, unburdened. She seemed happy but wary. "I warned him enough was enough."

"Damn right."

"I need to figure some things out. About the restaurant, about Katherine."

Carter nodded. Not an easy knot to untangle. He wished he had more help to offer than just threatening the jerk.

"Maybe speak to a lawyer," he said, to say something.

Ivana put a hand on Carter's shoulder. "I wanted to say thank you. You really gave me the courage to do it. I'd never seen him scared before. Once I saw him like that...he wasn't so scary to me."

Carter patted her hand. "Glad I could help a little, but you have the courage to do it. I know you can figure it out."

"Well, thank you."

He left the change behind for her and carried the bag outside.

Back at the truck, they decided it smelled too good to wait for the drive home, so they ate in the cab. They settled into a long stretch of no talking and only happy eating sounds. Finally, Bree broke the silence.

"So," she said. "When did you decide to become a killer?"

Carter stopped chewing. The food suddenly tasted sour. He swallowed and washed it down with a sip of his drink. He spoke while staring out the windshield into the trees at the far end of the parking lot.

"The man, Justin, your neighbor, he was responsible for my daughter's death."

"Oh, wow. He killed her?"

"Not directly, like took her into the woods and shot her. But he was responsible."

Bree nodded. "And he got away with it."

Carter nodded an affirmative and took a sip of his drink. It was sweet, creamy, and reminded him of his dinners with Ava.

"I felt like things needed to be put right."

"I get it," she said.

He wasn't thrilled to be talking about it, but it beat the alternative topic of his impending expiration date.

"And you think taking care of your brother will put things right with you?"

Bree set down her drink on the dashboard and thought a moment. "I think it's like...there's this wall in front of me, and it's too tall to climb. I need figure out some way through. I've been digging at it and chipping away, but I know I won't be able to do it alone."

"And you don't want to do it yourself? With him, I mean."

"I don't think I could."

Carter chuckled. "I didn't think so either."

"I've thought about it. I mean, I carry a knife just in case, y'know, I need to protect myself. But I don't know how to do it and not get caught."

"Someone your age shouldn't have to carry that weight their whole life anyway. I've only had this burden a few days, and I can tell you, it'll weigh you down."

"Yeah, that too. When I leave, I want to make a clean break, not run away, y'know?"

He nodded slowly. The people in the restaurant, they weren't scared of him. Neither was this girl, and she had every reason to be. She'd seen him kill. He knew what he did to Justin didn't make up even a small percentage of who he really was.

"I'm not some hitman."

Bree leaned in close, the heat from her take-out container of food pushing steam up around her face as she spoke. "No, you're someone who knows when somebody needs to be taken care of. You're someone who likes helping people. You're someone who understands justice. You're someone who can do what needs to be done."

He let himself get carried away in her sales pitch for a moment, but he knew it was exactly that—a sales job.

"Bree…"

"Does he need to start beating me? Is that it? Did I tell you what he almost did to Katy?"

"Your brother is a jerk; you get no argument from me there. I just don't know how all this sits on me yet. I don't want to become that guy."

"What guy? The hero?"

"You know what I mean." He took another bite. The truck seemed very small and shrinking every minute.

"So…are you gonna do this or not?"

He let out a long breath of air, and closed the empty take-out container.

"I just don't know if I'm ready to be that guy. You do something once and it can be a lone act. A mistake or an experiment or something you try to just see what it's like. But you do it twice…you're committing to something."

"Carter, this isn't trying pot once or seeing if you look good in bangs. You could help me and Katy and get rid of someone truly shitty in the world. That all sounds like a good thing to me."

"Yeah, to *you*. Of course, it sounds good to you. You don't have to pull the trigger."

"You said yourself you don't have much time left. Do you want that time to mean something?"

He shook his head and turned away from her. "Don't do that. You can't sit there at, what? Eighteen? And tell me at seventy-two that what I do now is the thing that's gonna give my life a purpose."

Bree crumpled the bag around her leftovers and tossed it on the dash. "I'm nineteen."

"And at nineteen, nobody knows shit about the world. Especially if they've never gone more than fifty miles from home."

Her eyes went dark. Her hands clenched into fists, and she lifted her feet to rest against the glove box. "That's exactly what I'm trying to avoid. I don't want to be stuck here. I don't want to know nothing. I want to live a life, not just an existence. I'm a hundred and twenty pounds of dead weight right now. I mean no more than a pile of leaves in the yard. I haven't done anything or seen anything, and all I wanted was a goddamn chance."

Carter hung his head. He felt awful for what he'd said, even though he believed the sentiment behind it. "Let me take you back."

He drove slowly. When he reached the end of the block, he looked back toward Mesa Grande. A new car was in the lot, and he saw a man moving toward the front door. A man he recognized.

Carter braked and turned sharply into the lot. He stayed at the back, pulling all the way forward so they could no longer see the front door.

"What're you doing?" Bree asked.

"I saw someone."

He held out a quieting hand and tried to crane his neck to see, but he had to get out if he wanted a clear view. "You wait here. Seriously, don't get out."

Carter hurried away from the truck and watched the man stagger forward. He was right. Eddie, and he looked drunk.

Carter moved forward quickly and fell in behind him. Eddie reached the bottom of the three concrete steps up to the door of the restaurant. He could see Ivana behind the counter inside.

"Fucking bitch," he slurred almost to himself, but Carter was close enough behind to hear. He decided quickly that no good could come of Eddie going inside. Carter put a hand on Eddie's shoulder. Eddie spun quickly, knocking Carter back a step and off balance.

"You," Eddie said. "You prick. Who the fuck are you to put your foot in another man's marriage?"

Carter steadied himself, not sure if he was ready for a fight with a drunk and emboldened Eddie.

"Eddie, you gotta go home, man." Carter didn't want him driving anymore, but didn't want him here even more.

"Are you sweet on her? Is that it?"

"Eddie, let's go."

"No," Eddie said. "Bitch gotta learn."

Carter sighed. He didn't want it to come to this, and he had no weapons, no dog, and Eddie was not going to be intimidated like last time.

"Eddie, don't."

Eddie put a hand on the railing. Inside, Ivana saw him, and her face went white. She stepped back and bumped into the counter behind her.

"I showed that little bitch daughter of hers already. Time to teach Mama Bear a lesson."

Carter felt his blood go hot. It raced through him like a scalding jolt from a live wire. He took three steps forward, put a hand on Eddie's shoulder, and pulled. Eddie tipped from the step and fell backward. His impaired state didn't let him catch his balance before he hit the asphalt of the parking lot. He wheezed out air from his lungs. Carter stood over him and straddled. He put a knee on Eddie's sternum and punched him once in the face.

Carter pulled his hand back with a yelp of pain. "God dammit." He thought there was a good chance he might have broken something. Eddie looked none the worse for the punch, though he was dazed.

"You're gonna get out of here, Eddie, and you're not gonna come back. Ever. You hear me?"

"Fuck you."

Eddie squirmed under him, but Carter pushed down harder on his ribcage. Eddie grunted and wrapped his hands around Carter's knee.

Carter twisted away and stood. He knew Eddie would take a moment to get back on his feet. He jogged back to the truck and pulled open the passenger door. Bree inhaled sharply in shock.

Carter met Bree's eye. "You said you had a knife?"

She flinched. He held out his hand, palm open. "Do you have it?"

Bree reached into her pocket and took out her knife. It was a short blade—three and a half inches—serrated like tiny shark's teeth. She thumbed it open with the circular hole on the blade, then turned it and handed the black plastic grip to Carter.

Too small to intimidate too much, but Carter didn't intend to threaten Eddie with it.

He slammed the door closed and jogged back to where Eddie now stood with one hand on the handrail leading to the front door.

"Hey," he said. Eddie turned and, in one motion, took a swing at Carter. Carter jerked out of the way, and the momentum spun Eddie around, and he fell again. Carter bent down to where he lay on the gravel. He leaned back and stabbed down into Eddie's thigh. Eddie thrashed, and Carter felt the blade moving under his skin, caught in the muscle. Eddie cried out, and his hands went to his leg, gripping his pants and clawing at the pain. Carter felt the blade scrape against bone.

"You're gonna leave, Eddie." Eddie's eyes were shut tight, spit leaking from the sides of his closed lips as he screamed into his mouth. "You're not gonna come back, right?"

When Eddie didn't answer, Carter twisted the knife, feeling it cut through more meat and the tip etching lines into the thigh bone. Eddie's only reply was another yowl of pain.

"Never coming back, right?"

Eddie couldn't seem to muster words, but he nodded. His face was red, and sweat beaded along his scalp line. Carter stood, pulling the blade out with him. Eddie let out a huge exhale accompanied by a scream and then went limp.

Carter threw a look back to the glass doors. Ivana mouthed to him, "It's okay. Just go."

He hurried back to the truck, the blade dripping blood as he went. He pulled open the door again, and he pushed the knife toward her. Bree took it and saw the blood.

"What the hell was that?"

Carter got behind the wheel. He gripped it tight and let out a long breath. He was sweating, rings forming under his arms, his hair damp.

"Some people won't ever learn, will they?"

Bree shook her head, eyes intent on the bloodstain on her knife blade.

"Some people only respond to a swift kick in the pants."

"Or something else," she said.

"Yeah."

She dug out a wad of napkins from the takeout bag and wiped the blade, then folded the knife and put it back in her pocket.

"You okay?" she asked.

"Yeah, I'm okay," Carter said. He dropped the truck in gear. "Let's see if Chris will learn."

He gunned the engine forward, and they drove away without Bree ever seeing what he'd done. She didn't seem to care. Her plan was moving forward. She smiled and finished the rest of her drink.

Eddie made her leave the exam room. Ivana had driven him to the ER, Eddie cursing the whole way in the passenger seat. When they checked in, it was easy to tell a lie about him accidentally dropping a knife into his leg in the restaurant. Eddie was either too embarrassed or too drunk to counter the lie. The nurse examining the wound took the story without question.

Eddie had called the junior doctor a string of cruel names when she injected him with Novocaine around the wound so she could clean it out and stitch it up. When Ivana had tried to calm him, that's when he kicked her out.

"Just go wait outside. You're not helping, goddammit."

The doctor wouldn't meet her eye as Ivana slunk out of the tiny exam room to take a chair on the other side of the thin curtain. She could still hear his angry rants and the doctor losing patience with him.

"What're you doing? You're s'possed to make it better," he slurred at her.

"It's quite deep, sir. I need to get it cleaned out so there's no risk of infection."

"Well, try to be careful, for fucks sake."

Ivana worried her hands in her lap. Her clothes still smelled like the kitchen at Mesa Grande, the scent of cooking spices even stronger than the antiseptic smells of the hospital.

She couldn't believe Carter would do such a thing, even if she'd fantasized about it for years. Her incredible willpower and self-control were the only things keeping Eddie safe from his wife, who worked in a room full of knives every day.

This regular customer, her longtime friend, had shown himself to be much more in recent weeks. She wished she could take some of his strength to stand up to Eddie, but she knew it wasn't likely.

Ivana heard him grunt and curse, and then the doctor admonished him, "Keep still, please."

"You're stabbing me with a fucking needle. What do you expect me to do?"

Ivana wondered if the doctor had started the stitches before the Novocaine had fully kicked in. And if she had, did she do it on purpose?

Either way, with each groan and swear word Eddie gritted out, Ivana smiled to herself. She couldn't help it.

Carter sat down opposite Ken and debated how much to tell him. He also wondered how much Ken would hear and if that's exactly why he came here in the first place.

Ken smiled when Carter showed up, nodded at him with a certain recognition in his eye, but he still hadn't used Carter's name.

"How you holding up?" Carter asked him.

"Well as ever," he said.

The puzzle on the table hadn't been filled in more than maybe twenty pieces of the five hundred spread out. Most of the top edge was done, but nothing in the middle, like the center of the idyllic world depicted on the box, had been carved out and left hollow.

"Things have been getting...crazy," Carter said.

"When are they not?"

"Crazier than normal, I guess."

"Crazy's good. Keeps it interesting."

Carter nodded slowly, worked his tongue over his teeth.

"I've found myself doing things I never thought I'd do."

Ken waved a hand that was little more than a collection of jumbled bones in a weathered glove of skin. "Doing things is better than doing nothing." He slapped his palms on the arms of his wheelchair. "Trust me. I don't do a goddamn thing all day. I wish I was out there doing things with you."

"What would you do if you were out with me?"

Ken took on the blankest expression Carter had ever seen in his life. The question had stumped him completely. After a long beat, Ken shrugged and looked away.

"How is it something can feel right and feel wrong at the same time?"

Ken kept his eyes turned away. "You ever feel like that's all life is? Asking questions that ain't got an answer? Not like we're too dumb to know or too dumb to figure it out, but they genuinely don't have an answer to them. And no point in looking for one, either."

"Yeah, you got something there." Carter reached over and snapped a piece of the puzzle into place. A tree. "Ken, I'm dying."

"Shit, we're all dying."

"Yeah, well, me faster than the rest of you."

Ken waved a hand across the room. "You think this is a race? There ain't no winners, I'll tell you that for sure."

"I just wanted you to know."

"Yeah, well, I'll see you on the other side."

They both smiled. "You know who I am?" Carter asked.

"I know who you are."

Carter didn't push it. He believed his old friend.

Detective DeFore had nothing.

He wasn't sure if it was the atrophy in his skills as a detective, or if it was that this case was destined to go in the cold pile from the start. Justin Lyons was such a non-entity that it gave the case very little foundation to build on.

The prison time was the obvious angle. Enemies made inside. DeFore had a list of anyone who got out recently who had spent time inside with Lyons. Some of those prison grudges lasted for years. Once you've been inside, you learn patience, if nothing else.

Chief Winters, so far, hadn't pressured him too much for results. If anything, having an active homicide case made the whole department feel more real, more big-time. This is the stuff they make TV shows about, not responding to a guy drunkenly showing his dick around a supermarket and shouting, "This is my light saber!"

But DeFore wanted results. He wanted to wrap the case, show he still had the chops. Maybe it was time to call in the help Chief Winters had offered. Or maybe it was time to admit he'd gotten rusty. Only way to deal with rust is to scrape it off, grease up the gears and get that engine moving again.

He wondered if he'd take that advice when it came to the rest of his life. Nine years now since his engagement fell apart, only a month out from the wedding. It wasn't his cold feet, but hers. He'd gone on dates since then, but few and far between. So far, at this point, he felt more rusty about women than he did about the homicide case in front of him.

It meant he lived alone, and he had time to spend on the case. No awkward calls to tell anyone he'd be working late. No angry partner at home getting pissed off as dinner grew cold on the table. Just him and the work. One case that could take all his focus. DeFore tried not to think about how goddamn depressing that was. He vowed that once this case was solved, he'd put himself out there again. Maybe join a dating site. If he could solve this, he had the perfect small talk for a first date. He'd be the guy who solved the Justin Lyons case.

He took another sip of coffee and went back to reading prison release records.

Bree counted her money again. This time, it felt like every dollar was another mile of road between her and this house. Each bill fluttered like a wing ready to carry her away.

She wanted to know how much Katy had squandered, how much of a deficit they had to make up. Getting rid of Chris was only step one. They still needed the cash to make it all the way to California. No reason to leave the snowy drifts of the northern Midwest only to stall out halfway across the Nevada desert. Bree didn't care if prostitution was legal there she wanted to start her own way, and that meant on her own two feet, not on her back.

She packed away the money, giving it one last deep sniff. Each bill had its own scent, its own pattern of wear from the hundreds of hands that touched them and spent them in their own pursuit of a dream, even if that dream only amounted to getting drunk that night or high or spiked on insulin from a candy bar.

Bree slid on her jacket, then walked out past the living room, avoiding Mama's eyes. Wheel Of Fortune was on. In all the years she'd seen Mama watch that stupid show, Bree had never seen Mama get one puzzle right. Too goddamn dumb.

"Hey, you," Mama said. So maternal. "Grab me a Dr. Pepper out of the fridge."

Bree didn't stop walking. "Get it yourself."

Out front, she saw Carter's truck parked halfway down the block. It was so hard not to look at it, to nod or give a wink, some signal that they were in on a plan together. But she kept her gaze fixed on her own car, parked nearly bumper to bumper with Chris's. Bree removed her jacket since the evening was warm. She got in, cranked the engine, and made sure to give his bumper a little tap when she pulled out. She drove past Carter's truck and stared straight ahead.

She made it to Katy's, finally not feeling like a bag of bricks weighed on her shoulders. The sky seemed a little brighter, the heat made just for her to warm the chill in her bones she'd lived with for so long.

Bypassing the front walk, she headed for Katy's window on the side of the house. She'd nearly worn a path through the tall grass. Two lines of sneaker prints tamped down the green and threatened to make a brown trail leading right under Katy's window.

When she got closer, she could hear Katy's dad. His familiar choked-off rage. Her steps slowed. He was yelling, and the words didn't matter. She'd heard them before, though not as many times as Katy. Bree knew immediately that Katy's mom would be at work, always at work.

Bree crouched under the window and listened. In the pauses when he sucked a deep breath to get the air to continue his tirade, Bree could hear Katy sobbing. The girl cried so much Bree was surprised she wasn't withered like a dried apple.

Bree curled her knees to her chest, all the excitement and hope from her drive over here instantly gone with a slap of reality. As bad as things were for Bree, she always knew it could be worse, and she needed only to look for Katy to see what worse looked like.

This goddamn world, full of mountains too tall to climb over, water too wide to swim across, walls and fences and roadblocks. Ropes and chains to bind you to the ground and keep you right where you are. Sometimes, all it took was words.

She listened, a pain inside her that she couldn't help. If she showed herself, if she tried to break in and defend Katy from whatever he was after her about, and Bree didn't even know this time, things would only go worse for Katy. She'd tried before. It was why she only came around to the window, and never thought the front door.

She unfolded her knife. Carter had let her inside to clean the blade before she left his house. He washed it in the sink to avoid Bree having to get any blood on her. She closed the knife, then thumbed it open again, then twice more. Carter may have it in him, but she did not. She put the knife back in her pocket.

Bree cried, but silently. Afraid to be overheard, but hoping her tears would join Katy's and float them both out of there.

Carter scratched at the whiskers on his chin, then followed the itch up his cheek to under his ear. He hadn't noticed them at first, coming in white the way they were. Ava had always preferred him clean-shaven, and he kept up the habit. Now, he wondered if he'd live long enough to see what he looked like with a full beard.

It had been a half-hour since Bree left, and still, Chris stayed inside. Carter had the window rolled down to let a breeze in, but the air outside was still and warm. He'd left Chester at home. Figured this was no job for a dog. A weird part of him didn't want Chester to have a negative opinion of him. The dog looked at Carter like he was his savior, and he didn't want that to change. Not that Chester would understand, but Carter would know what the dog saw, so it was easier for him to stay at home.

The screen door snapped open, and Chris came out. Carter sat up in his seat and gripped the wheel like a driver waiting for the green flag. He checked the gun case on the seat next to him, then waited for Chris to pull away. He let him take the first turn before following.

Tailing Chris was easy. He was either too stupid or too arrogant to think anyone would follow him without noticing. It got markedly harder once they headed out of town, and where they were, all roads led quickly out of town. Chris turned East on a two-lane country highway and headed into the fields. Carter stayed back a good mile, watching Chris's headlights rise and fall with the rolling hills. He was headed to the lakes—what the locals called this area. Fishing and some camping, if you could stand the mosquitoes, and not much else out here. Too marshy to build anything substantial on. A strange place for a drug deal.

Carter considered catching up to him and running him off the road, then gunning him down in the wreckage, but there were too many variables. Too many unknowns. Plus, he didn't want to damage his truck. He'd be damned if he was going to buy another vehicle this close to the end of the line.

The trees became more dense, and Carter could see flashes of the moon reflecting off pools of black water between the trees. Brake lights came on, and Chris turned left off the two-lane. Carter kept on and drove past, sneaking a look down the narrow dirt path where Chris had turned, and he saw some string lights hung between trees. A campsite, maybe?

Carter went another mile up the road and then turned around. He came back slowly, and when he saw the glow of the lights tucked into the trees, he turned off his headlights and let the soft dots of light lead him in.

He pulled off the highway but stopped as soon as his car wasn't immediately visible from the road, though not a single car had passed this way in ten minutes.

When he got out, he could hear the steady buzz of generators. He left the gun behind and went to scout the area. A quarter mile down the dirt road, he found a foursome of single-wide trailer homes arranged around a central area with an unlit fire pit. String lights hung all around the area, so the little compound was lit well, better than it looked from the road through the dense trees.

He could see Chris's car, along with three others, parked haphazardly around the lot. A few trees had been cleared, and the ground was tamped down from tires and feet. This had been here a while.

The constant noise of multiple generators—one per mobile home—masked any noise Carter made as he snuck around. He could smell the engines burning fuel, along with another smell not unlike burning gasoline. He deduced pretty quickly this was where the drugs were being made. In between county jurisdictions, away from prying eyes. The spot was ideal as long as you didn't get any curious fishermen dropping by. It was also the exact place the police would expect a drug dealer to get shot. Carter could hide the kill in plain sight, and the list of suspects would be as long as his arm before they got to an old man doing a favor for a teen girl he just met.

Carter went back to the truck and got the rifle. He came back through the trees and waited with a clear view of Chris's car.

"My fault? How the hell is it my fault?"

Every time Chris moved in the narrow trailer, the whole thing tipped to whatever side he stood on. Behind a desk centered in the room for maximum stability sat Dilbert "Dill" Reese, the same age as Chris but with a hard look under his shaved scalp and tattoos that crept up his arms and onto his neck.

"You blaming the product?" Dill asked. "Because famously, drugs kinda sell themselves."

"It's my fault if some kids decide to kick or the fucking economy tanks and they don't have the cash?"

"You better check the way you talk to me, man."

Chris scoffed. "Dill, we went to high school together. Stop trying to act all big boss man on me."

"I am the boss man."

Dill gave Chris an even stare. They were equals in many ways, yes, but Dill had the edge, and he knew it. He *was* the boss of this operation, and the only reason Chris was here was because of their history.

After grade school and middle school, being tortured about his name, Dill finally had enough and in the eight grade, began to fight back. He was ruthless. He cheated, he ambushed, he eye gouged, crotch kicked, and did whatever it took to get his point across. It took nearly a whole semester of ass-kickings, and he never once came out on the losing side. He wasn't that big, not too strong, but he was motivated, and the years of abuse had thickened his skin and dulled whatever empathy he might have for someone else's pain. He could go on in the face of someone begging for mercy and

123

keep punching until the lights went out.

He used his newfound status as someone not to be fucked with to go into the drug trade, dropped out of high school his senior year, and set himself up in his trailer park in the sticks. Chris hadn't ever made fun of his name, so he was hired.

"Okay, fine," Chris said. "I'll move a hundred percent of this product and move it quick. I can sell, man. Don't ever question that."

"Just don't forget whose name is on the door."

"Nobody's name is on the door, Dill. That'd be petty fucking stupid. You wanna put up golden arches like you're fucking McDonald's or something? Get the cops all over your ass."

Dill's patented death stare had been enough since his semester of pain to do the job of a steel-toed boot to the teeth, and when he shot it at Chris, he wilted.

"It's cool, Dill, it's cool. Shit, man. Sorry."

"Maybe you're giving out too many free samples."

Chris smiled, tried to charm his way out of the uncomfortable air in the tight little trailer.

"Hey, Dill, man, we gotta give 'em a taste of what we're selling."

"And if that means Cash Money gets a pretty young thing to drop her drawers for a sample, that's just the cost of business, right?"

Chris kept pacing, the trailer rocking back and forth. "You gotta spend money to make money, right?"

Dill always sat. He stood for no man. "The fuck does that even mean?"

"I don't know. It's shit people say."

"Well, don't say it around here. Take your shit and sell it. Be back for more in five days. That's how this shit works. You can't move that much; maybe you should be slinging burgers like your sister."

"Yo, fuck that."

Chris lifted a brick of cellophane-wrapped product off one of the desks they had stolen from the high school. Big steel beasts that would look at home on a battleship. All the furnishings—desks, file cabinets, trash baskets, staplers, coffee machine—had all come from late-night raids of their old alma mater.

"I'll see you next week."

"Sooner is okay, too."

"You know it, Dill."

The trailer swayed as Chris stepped down and threw the balance off. He carried the package of drugs like a football to his car. The three other trailers were busy cooking next week's supply. Chris rarely saw anyone go in or out, and when he did, they were dressed in hazmat suits. Every time he saw them, he thanked a God he didn't believe in that he wasn't stuck out here in the woods cooking crank. Maybe it was because Dill knew he nearly flunked out of Chemistry. Out on the street, finding pretty young things to be his next customers, was where Chris belonged.

He headed down the long dirt road toward the two-lane, tapping his steering wheel along to the hip hop on the stereo. His headlights swept across something in his way. Chris jammed on the brakes and said, "Fuck."

It was a man. An old man. He looked lost, like he ran away from a nursing home or something. Then he lifted a rifle in his hands and aimed it at Chris through the windshield.

Carter squeezed the trigger before he could lock eyes with the boy. The windshield spider-webbed and looked like cracked ice on a frozen lake. He saw that he hit Chris, but also saw the boy duck down behind the dashboard. Carter couldn't tell where he'd hit him. The car rocked on its shocks a little, so someone inside was still moving.

Carter stepped forward and levered in another round. He realized he was standing in the bright light of Chris's headlights. He shuffle-stepped aside, trying to keep the gun aimed, but it was hard without his feet planted.

The driver's door opened, and Chris tumbled out. He brought a sound with him of panic and pain. He hit the dirt and rolled. Carter tried to line up another shot. Chris's twisting and turning made Carter dizzy. He fired before it got worse. Chris fell hard into the dirt, then flopped on his back. Carter was breathing hard now, anxious about taking more than one shot. The generators could cover a lot of noise, but not rifle rounds.

Chris was in the shadows, only a faint glow of headlights wrapped around the front of the car to where he lay barely moving on the ground.

Carter took a slow step forward. He saw Chris's hand move, then saw the flash. The sound of the shot came at him like an echo of his own shots, and he dropped. One moment he was standing, and the next he was face down in the dead leaves and dirt, a stinging pain in his leg. As Carter went down, the lights hanging over the trailer compound went dark. In his tumble, he threw his arms out to catch himself and sent the rifle flying into the dark.

Now, the only lights in the stand of trees were Chris's headlights. All Carter could see of the boy were the bottoms of his feet, but they were still.

His wild shot seemed to be his last act.

Carter heard movement from the trailers. He was a fool to think Chris wouldn't be armed, and he wouldn't make that mistake twice. He knew there would be guns in the trailers and men who knew how to use them.

Carter tried to stand. His leg buckled. A hot pain bore through his thigh. He felt blood run down his leg as the realization settled over him that he'd been shot. He had no experience and no way to evaluate how bad the wound was, but the adrenaline and fear shut out most of the pain. He tried scanning the trees for his gun, but the darkness was total. He still saw tiny stars in his eyes from the muzzle flash of Chris's gun. There were shouts from within the compound. People headed his way.

He dragged himself off the dirt road and into the moss and mud-coated ground between the trees. No more shots came from Chris, and never would again. Carter moved to where he knew he'd parked the truck. He pulled his left leg behind him, as inanimate as a tree branch dragging in the dirt. He reached the passenger side of his truck and muscled himself in. He slid across the bench, pushing aside the empty gun case, and cranked the engine to life. Sweat soaked his face, and his breathing came shallow and ragged.

He kept the lights off as he used Chris's headlights as a guide to where the road was. He got the truck onto the road and stopped for a moment to look in the rearview. Bathed in red brake lights, Chris lay flat on his back, unmoving.

Satisfied, Carter hit the gas. A spasm of pain boiled up from his leg and through his whole body. But he was used to shivers of pain. The blood was new, but at least it was warm.

THREE

"Two in one week? Have we ever had two at once?"

Homicide detective Brian DeFore took the file handed to him by detective Hector Nava. A single page, double-spaced, with very little info on it.

"And get this," Nava said. "Also shot with a rifle round."

DeFore paused before sitting, nodded in acknowledgment that it could be significant.

"Same gun?"

"Don't know yet. Waiting on ballistics. He just came in."

DeFore sat, glanced over the one page. "Says he was dumped?"

"Yeah. No blood at the scene. No shell casing. Looks like he was killed somewhere else, dumped DOA."

Hector Nava had joined DeFore to help out when DeFore had run into a brick wall in Justin Lyons' murder investigation. They'd split the prison records search, knocked on a few doors, and come up with nothing. Lyons was getting colder by the day. This, though, this heated things up.

"Looks like we're a team a little longer then. Who'd have thought homicide was a two-man operation in this county? I just assumed on a life working alone."

Nava smiled. "Don't mean to cramp your style." Nava folded his hands over his overstuffed pillow of a belly. He'd gone soft since he left the street and joined the burglary unit, but had a keen nose for detective work, so anytime DeFore had his help, it was appreciated.

"Don't sweat it. As long as shoplifters and car thieves can live without you for a while."

"I think the department will make do."

DeFore stood and went to the machine in the corner for some coffee. Unlike most departments, Chief Winters had sprung for the good coffee machines so his crew would stop taking so much time away from their desks at Starbucks. Now, the stuff they brewed in-house was better than the stuff they charged you five bucks a cup for.

"Found out a little more about our man Justin Lyons," DeFore said.

"Vic number one."

DeFore turned and raised his eyebrows. "Hey, we never had a number two before."

"What a day." Nava laid on the sarcasm. "The thing you found out wouldn't happen to be who killed him, is it?"

"No, but it may give us a motive." DeFore sipped his coffee, smacked his lips with a satisfied smile.

"Do tell," Nava said.

"Well, you know Lyons did a stint in prison."

"Yeah."

"Turns out since he got sprung, he was supplementing his string of shitty minimum wage jobs with a little check fraud on the side. Now that he is deceased, a little bit of digging turned up twelve victims over the years."

Nava watched DeFore walk back to his desk. "And you think one of these people got wise and killed him?"

"I'm just saying maybe. It's a motive anyway."

"How much did he get?"

"A few grand each one before he'd get figured out, and they'd close the account."

Nava screwed up his face with doubt. "And you think someone killed him over a few grand?"

"Hey, my first year on the force, I had a guy who killed a dude over a pizza."

"A pizza?"

DeFore nodded. "A guy used to hang out around pizza joints and wait for names to be called. If they called the name twice he figured the people hadn't shown up yet so he stepped in and said, 'yeah, I'm Mr. Monroe' or whatever. Well, this one time, he gets his free pizza and, on his way out the door, bumps into the real Mr. Monroe. When the kid behind the counter says he just gave away Mr. Monroe's pizza, he's like, 'To who?' and the kid points to our pizza thief. Mr. Monroe runs him down, they argue, and he pulls a gun and shoots him. And a pizza's what, twelve bucks? You can buy a lot of pizza with a few grand."

Nava shook his head. "Still…"

"Hey, it's something."

"Well, this vic number two, Christopher Mercer, ought to turn up a whole lot of motive. This kid was a pretty well-known dealer in narcotics and fake IDs."

"Could be a drug gang beef. Like in the city?"

"Could be."

"Or could be a jealous girlfriend."

"Could be that too."

DeFore set aside his coffee and picked up the one-sheet on Chris. "Big thing now is to see if it's the same rifle and if these two knew each other."

"If the vics are related, we got ourselves a regular crime spree."

"Like cousins or something? Could be."

Nava shook his head. "No, I mean the killings are related, not the vics."

"Oh. Shit. Yeah. See, when I work alone, I never misunderstand what I'm saying."

"That's cause you talk to yourself."

"I know," DeFore smiled. "And I always make perfect sense to me."

The men both laughed. When it died down, DeFore said, "Okay, so we wait on ballistics, and in the meantime, we find out a little more about our two vics."

Nava couldn't help grinning. "Two. Damn. Two at once."

"Wish I shared your enthusiasm."

"No, I mean…just that there's two at once. Not that we have two murders. It's just…"

"I know what you mean. I'll feel better when we have two solved at once, though."

Carter woke up on the couch. Sometime in the night, he'd lost most of the real estate to Chester, who curled next to his head. The painkillers the doctor prescribed came in handy last night, and he'd taken two. Every year, every day of his seventy-two years pressed down on Carter's shoulders. He felt each hour he'd lived like a brick to carry.

He looked down at his leg, which was hanging off the couch. The quick bandage job was still in place, the blood stains gone dark and dry. No new blood flowing, which was a good sign. He shifted, and a jolt of pain grabbed his leg. The bullet may have gone all the way through and missed the bone, but it was still a gunshot, and it hurt like hell.

"Made it seventy-two years without one," he said out loud. "Couldn't make it six months more, god dammit."

Chester stirred and lifted his head. He was more alert than normal at this hour, watching Carter as he struggled to stand. A low whimper escaped the dog's throat.

"Don't worry about it," Carter said. "It's a little stiff from a night half on and half off the couch." He gave the dog a scowl, and Chester licked his lips, eyes still alert.

When Carter stumbled in the door last night, Chester was already awake and barking. Carter hadn't yet seen the coon hound's notorious vocal abilities, but Chester seemed to know something was wrong. He circled and jumped at Carter as he tried to get inside and settle into a chair.

Chester whined like his dinner was late while Carter rinsed the wound and wrapped it in an old t-shirt he cut up with scissors. When Carter finally opened the back door to let Chester out, the old dog stopped at the doorway, looked back over his shoulder, and waited until Carter gave him permission. He sat out on the porch and Chester made his fastest backyard run ever, then returned to Carter's side and didn't leave it the rest of the night.

He'd made a mess of it. Lost his gun, taken a bullet, alerted everyone in the trailer compound to his presence. Didn't seem like anyone saw him or followed him, though. That was good. His leg, however, was not good at all.

He knew they reported gunshots at the hospital, but he felt fairly certain he'd need stitches. Then again, who did he have to look pretty for? Damn the scar. If he could just nurse it along and make sure nothing got infected, he'd be fine.

"Seems goddamn ridiculous to work this hard to stay alive," he said to Chester. He hobbled to the hall closet and got out a broom, which he wedged under his armpit as a crutch. He limped to the back door and let Chester roam.

The morning had just broken, and the birds sounded, the insects sought newly open flowers, and the dew slowly lost its jewels to the sun. Another day. Carter knew he should appreciate each one, but it was hard to do with this throb in his leg. He'd get coffee, feed Chester, then take another pill. Maybe two.

Somewhere, Ava had a sewing kit, but he doubted it would come to that. "I'd probably pass out."

He knew a lot of people who got to his age and lamented all the things in life they never got to experience. He could check off a few more things from the list. Get shot? Check. Kill a man in cold blood? Check and check.

He reminded himself that Chris was not a good person. Selling those kids drugs was no different than Justin loading Audrey into his car and taking her away. The drug-addled kids might be dying a more slow-motion death, but the result was the same.

Chester returned to the back porch, gave one last look out at the yard and its enticing sounds and smells, then walked past Carter inside.

Carter fed him and made himself coffee. He sat in his armchair with a groan and propped his leg up on the coffee table.

"Not sure if I should be doing hot or cold compress, or if any of it matters a whit."

Chester looked at him like he wanted to help, but didn't know how.

"Guess I should at least change the dressing." He looked at the broom that he'd left across the room, using the back of the sofa to get him where he sat now. "In a minute."

Despite the coffee, Carter was asleep again soon after.

Bree lay in bed wide awake. She listened for sounds that Chris had come home, but the house was quiet, a rare state. She stood and pulled on yesterday's clothes. She listened at her door for a moment and then crept into the hall. Chris's door was closed, as it always was whether he was in or out. She walked down the hall and past the living room, where Mama was sprawled in her recliner. Bree peeked out the window, pushing the blinds open with two fingers.

Chris's car was not there.

All of this signaled good news for her. As she let herself think the deed was done and all that it meant for her and Katy, a police cruiser pulled to a stop in front of the house. She let her fingers go, and the blinds snapped shut. Bree padded quickly on bare feet back to her room.

She listened at the door for the knock. It came loud and sharp. It had to be to wake up Mama. Bree heard her shout, "Who is it?," then the reply, "Police, ma'am. Can you open the door, please?"

"Breanna!"

Damn it. The fat, lazy witch was going to make her do this. It would put her at risk if her acting wasn't good enough, the level of shock and surprise insufficient enough to make her a suspect. But what did she do? She didn't pull the trigger. She didn't pay to have it done. She was clean.

"Breanna! The door!"

Bree stepped into the hallway and faked a yawn. No, too much. Don't do that in front of the cops.

"What, Mama?"

"Police at the door."

When Bree came into the room, she saw genuine fear on Mama's face. It surprised her. But with Chris being Chris, they both expected this knock at the door someday, with or without Bree's help.

Bree answered, but only opened the door a tiny bit.

Two blue-suited officers stood on the steps. They'd removed their hats. "Is this the home of Christopher Mercer?"

Mama immediately started crying. Bree said, "Yes."

"May we come inside, please?"

Bree held open the door, and the two officers stepped in with somber looks on their faces. They didn't need to say a word. Both Mama and Bree knew the news they were there to deliver, but for different reasons.

"He's dead. Dear lord, he's dead, isn't he?" Mama's bellow filled the room. She lunged to one side to throw herself out of the chair, about the only way she could get out of it these days. The recline lever had been broken and permanently set in the full lay-back position for years. Bree used to joke with Katy that they shouldn't call it a Lay-Z-Boy since it obviously works with lazy women just as well.

Bree drifted back in shuffling steps to the kitchen. Mama's histrionics took all the attention of the policemen. She got herself out of the chair and knocked over her TV tray in the process, spilling a half-full Dr. Pepper on the carpet.

Bree watched it all with remove, like it was a TV show. She barely heard the words over Mama's wailing, but they told her Chris had been found dead, shot twice. They were investigating but had no leads yet, and did she know of anyone who might have done it. Mama told them nothing.

The officer who'd knocked came over to Bree. "How about you, ma'am? Do you know of anyone with any reason to kill Christopher?"

It was odd to hear his full name.

"Look, I'm sure you know he wasn't exactly a saint."

"We're aware he had some arrests."

"Yeah, well, that wasn't the half of what he was into. I can't say I'm surprised to hear this, but specific people who might want to kill him? No. I tried hard not to mix with any of Chris's friends."

It was a last-minute decision to go with hard indifference over grief, but Mama was selling enough grief for the both of them, so anything Bree would have faked would have seemed like a B-movie performance. So she was honest.

"Do you mind if we have a look in his bedroom?"

"Have at it." She pointed the way. One officer stayed with Mama, trying to console her. Bree wondered if Mama would be this upset if someone came to the door and told her that her only daughter was dead. Bree doubted it very much.

She snuck out without telling Mama, who hadn't stopped weeping well after the cops had gone. Bree got into her car and cranked the engine, imagining what it would be like when she finally started up and drove West for good, no looking back. Maybe she could have Chris's car now that he wouldn't be needing it anymore. Not like she had a lot to take with her. Storage wasn't an issue.

She drove toward Carter's house in the farmlands. She hummed with nervous energy and had to talk to someone about it, and he was the only one. It killed her not to be able to tell Katy, but she knew it was too risky. But she needed to get it out, to talk about what it meant to her, how scared she was, how excited, how happy. She'd had less of a buzz after a two-liter bottle of Mountain Dew. When she passed out of town, and the air began to smell like freshly tilled soil and cow manure, somehow, it had never smelled sweeter.

It could have been a beautiful house with some paint, a few repairs. Carter seemed so alone, though. She understood why he wouldn't want to get on a ladder and fix a broken shutter. And sometimes, it's easier to let something go than to fix it. It's what Bree was doing with her whole life here in Bellington.

His truck was in the driveway, faded red. Old, like him. This white-haired man, a real killer, and she was excited to go and see him. Talk to him about the deed.

Bree knocked on the door and heard Chester bark from inside. If she didn't already know what a sweet marshmallow he was, his bark would have

141

been intimidating.

"Who is it?" Carter called.

"It's Bree."

He thought she heard him say, "Aw, shit," nice and low, but then he called out, "It's open."

She pushed inside and saw Carter on the couch, his leg up and wrapped in a cloth with dark stains on it. Chester barked at her a few times but didn't leave Carter's side. The old man stayed on the couch, trying to adjust himself and sit up straighter, but every movement made his face scrunch up and wrinkle.

"What happened?"

He let himself fall back onto the couch, giving up on finding a comfortable position. He sighed heavily. "I got shot a little bit."

Bree moved across the room. "A *little bit*? Let me see."

Carter held out his hands to keep her away from his leg, but she got right up close to it and examined the bandage. "Did he do this to you?"

"Yeah."

"Mother fucker."

"I was shooting at him at the time. All's fair, I guess."

"Are you okay?"

"I will be, after a time. Hurts like the devil, though."

She stood straight over him. Chester's tail began wagging.

"Do you need a hospital?"

"Can't," he said. "They report gunshot wounds."

"Isn't that just something they say on TV?"

"You willing to find out?"

Bree cocked a hip to one side, thinking. "Well, god dammit."

"Yeah."

"At least let me re-do the dressing for you. Looks like you tied it off with an old t-shirt."

"It is an old t-shirt."

She started walking toward the kitchen. "Jesus Christ, Carter. Do you want to get infected and lose your leg?"

142

She opened cabinets and checked in drawers, but nothing looked like it could help him. "Don't you have a first aid kit or something?" she called.

"Never had call for one before. I got some Band-Aids."

She came back into the living room. "Band-Aids on a bullet wound. Great." She moved for the door. "I'll go out and get you something."

"No, no." He tried to sit up again, flopped back down. "It might look suspicious."

"Carter, people buy medical supplies. I'll get some gauze, some hydrogen peroxide. That kinda stuff."

"I don't know."

"I'll pay cash. Just relax." Bree walked out.

Carter felt the air push down on him, heavier than before. It may have been the rising humidity as summer loomed, but to him, it felt like the weight of what he'd done, a burden he would bear for the rest of his short life. A weight pushing him deeper into a grave that opened at his feet the moment the doctor told him there was no hope.

But hope came in different forms. Hope sometimes comes as a red-headed girl who needed his help. Hope was a gift he could give now that his was all used up.

She came back a short time later and set about re-dressing his wound. Carter felt odd having this girl working on his thigh. She made him take his pants off, and she smiled at his tight white drawers.

"At least they don't have holes in them," she said.

"Ava was a stickler."

"Well, lucky me, she burned it into you. This is the classic Mom scenario of 'Don't get caught needing medical attention without clean underwear.'"

Carter took one of the pain pills while she was gone, anticipating the hurting she was going to put on him while changing the bandage. She did not disappoint. Bree had little in the way of bedside manner. She stripped off the t-shirt and didn't slow down when she came to parts where the dried blood made it stick to his leg. The holes began slowly weeping blood when she had removed the old stained rag. She doused both entry and exit wounds in peroxide, and the skin around the holes bubbled white.

"See?" she said. "Infection."

Bree only seemed to pause in her ham-fisted nursing attempts when Carter bent at the waist and let out a low grunt.

"Shit, sorry," she said.

"Not you," he managed to grit out through his teeth. The pain pill blunted the cramp in his insides his disease put on him, but when your whole body ties in a knot from the inside, no amount of medication could be enough.

Bree leaned back, gauze and tape in one hand, ready to dress his wound.

"It'll pass," he said.

They waited it out, and slowly, the cramp faded, and Carter unfolded his body.

"Sorry. Just my body reminding me what's to come."

"You really are sick, huh?"

"You thought I was joking?"

"Yeah, well, so far, you're not that funny, so maybe."

She slathered on a gel disinfectant and re-wrapped his leg tightly with gauze and then an Ace bandage on top of that to hold it all in place. He expected his toes to turn blue any minute at the lack of blood flow, but the pill was working its magic, so he leaned back on the couch, covered himself with a blanket, and exhaled. Bree gave him a bottle of Coke to sip.

She sat in the armchair and scratched Chester's ears. He'd been banished from the couch while she worked, but it didn't stop him from nosing in and checking what she was doing like a worried parent. Now, he responded to her touch with a low groan.

Bree watched Carter, looking frail as his age, finally. But he'd shown he still had some kick left in him. "So you did it."

Carter nodded and set the Coke on the table in front of him. "I did."

"The police came to the house."

He closed his eyes and listened to her. She stayed quiet for a long while, Chester's grumbles filling the space. Her excitement and electric energy had faded from when she first arrived. She spoke quietly now.

"Thank you. I'm sorry you got shot."

"Perils of the job," he said and then let out a laugh that was mostly the pill talking.

"I'm serious, Carter. What you did for me is huge. And I'm gonna make sure you get better. I'll look after you."

Carter thought about Audrey, how it was her job to tend to her old father. And he knew she would have never complained. A devoted daughter. Of course, she'd probably have her own family by now. Kids, a husband who loved her like Carter loved Ava. But she'd always make time for Daddy.

Silent tears trickled from the corners of his eyes. He wasn't sure how much was the drugs and how much was the pain of missing her that hadn't seemed to fade at all over the decades.

"You deserve it," he said. "Deserve a chance."

"You think so?"

"Everyone does. Nobody else should ever get to take away your chance at a life. Nobody."

The wrapping was snug on his leg and he felt comfortable for the first time lying down. He felt his mind drift toward sleep. In the fog, he saw the redhead girl and Audrey fade into each other.

"I'm gonna make the most of this opportunity, Carter. I swear to you, I am."

"All anyone needs is a chance." He smacked his lips and took a sip of Coke. "You get that chance, you make the best of it and let the chips fall where they will."

He turned his head and forced his eyes open. They were wet, red. She met his gaze and didn't look away. She listened closely.

"It won't always work out, kid. Things go bad. But in the end, things balance out. And someday, we all go to sleep, and don't wake up. And after that...after that..."

He closed his eyes again, settled his head on the pillow, and drifted off.

Bree sat watching him for a long time, rubbing Chester until he dozed off as well.

"I never knew my grandpa," she said, though she knew Carter was sleeping. She just needed to talk. "But I wish he was like you, Carter."

Cicada song rose and fell as wind blew steady through the trees. Bree watched Chester chase through the tall grass, his nose working overtime to seek out the smells riding on the breeze. Earlier, the dog had started walking in circles, and he nosed her hand, so Bree got the hint and let him out. Carter was still asleep on the couch.

She looked out over the undeveloped land. The old bones of farmland were still there, buried under overgrowth, but it was nice not to see houses or hear neighbors. The land was pretty around here, and she started to think it wasn't this town at all that she hated and wanted to get away from, but the people she was trapped inside with. Outside, things were more possible. But inside her house, the Burger Barn, Katy's house—they were each their own stifling cage.

Her mind was open, and for the moment, there was peace, and then the realization came crashing in of what she had done to Chris. She had killed her brother, set the machine in motion, and now he was dead. Mama was crushed. Carter was shot.

Like a summer squall, the tears fell from her eyes, and she dropped to her knees and wept while Chester cut paths through the tall grass.

She fed the dog from a can she found in a kitchen cupboard. The sun had fallen, and she knew she should get home, but the house was so wonderfully quiet. No TV blaring, no hip-hop beats shaking the walls. She didn't know any of the art on the walls or the people in the photos, but it all felt familiar somehow. Same with the furniture. Everything was just so and exactly where it should be. Not the kind of house anyone would put on TV, and if one of those Home and Garden shows ever did come here, they'd have a mile-long list of things to change, walls to knock down, colors to cover what was here. But in that moment, to Bree, it was perfect.

Carter had begun to stir, the pill wearing off. She turned on a lamp in the living room and waited for him to wake. Chester came from the kitchen licking his chops, went straight to Carter and licked the side of his face with a tongue still coated in dog food. Carter jerked awake to find Bree laughing at him.

"Did I fall asleep?"

"For about three hours."

He looked around, noticed the dark.

"You hungry?" she asked.

Carter stretched and winced when his leg reminded him of the pain. "No, I'm okay."

"Let me get you something to drink anyway." Bree turned and went for the kitchen.

"A beer?" he said.

"Okay."

She came back with a can of beer and set it on the coffee table for him. He sat up, keeping his leg straight.

"How's it feel?"

"Stiff," he said.

"Can I check it?"

"You know first aid or something?"

"Just basics. I kinda had to fend for myself a lot growing up."

Carter laughed. "Growing up. I love when kids your age say stuff like that."

"I'm nineteen. That's grown up."

He chuckled again and cracked the top of his beer. "Girl, you have a whole lot of growing up still to do."

She made a sour face as he took a sip. He swallowed quickly and wiped his mouth.

"It's not a bad thing," Carter said. "The hardest part is over. At least you hope so."

"You think?"

"For most people, yeah. At least now you get to steer your own ship."

"I'll settle for driving my own car. Speaking of…" Bree looked around the room to see if there was anything else she could do. "I should take off."

"Yeah, me too."

She furrowed her brow at him. "Where the hell do you think you're going?"

"I need to go get that gun. It's not good if it's out there." He moved as if to get up, but his face contorted in pain. Bree walked to him with her arms out, ready to push him down, but he fell back on his own.

"You're not going anywhere."

Carter looked out the window. "Shit. Too damn dark anyway."

"Yeah, and you can't be rooting around in the woods on that leg."

He let out a long exhale. "Okay. Not today. But I want to go find it anyway."

"Leave it. It's done."

"It was my father's."

She jolted a little, worried. "Can they trace it back to you?"

"Doubtful. It's real old. Before modern gun registry and all that. Been in the family since before I was born." She made a face like *woah, that is a long time.* "Still want it back, though. Even just on principle."

"You don't think the guys out at the trailers have it by now?"

"Maybe. Still…"

Bree grinned. "I get it. You're stubborn like me." She grabbed a crumpled throw blanket off the back of the armchair and tossed it to Carter. "Can I trust you to stay in tonight?"

He nodded with a smile. "Hey, thanks. Really."

"I'll be back tomorrow to check on that leg."

"You don't have to."

"Yes, I do. I don't think Chester is gonna do it."

Carter smiled. "He likes you."

"I like him too. He's fed and went out."

"Thanks."

"Okay. See you tomorrow."

As she walked to her car, she thought how very unlike a killer and client they seemed to her. In one day, she realized there was more good here than she knew and more darkness in plain sight than she ever imagined.

"I knew it. Same gun."

DeFore slapped down a manila folder in front of Nava, who jumped at the sudden interruption to his online records search.

"No shit?"

"No shit. A rifle. Same markings. You know how long it would have taken ballistics in the city, how busy they are?"

"No."

"A hell of a lot longer. But now color me intrigued by this thing. Two murders by the same gun in the same week."

Nava's chair squeaked as he rotated to follow DeFore's manic pacing of the room.

"You think it's like a serial thing?"

"Nah. That's thinking like a TV show. But they have to be related somehow, right?"

Nava gestured to his screen. "So far, I have no connection at all between the two vics, other than they were neighbors."

"That's gotta be something, right? No such thing as coincidences. Not like that." DeFore stopped behind his desk, still standing. He tapped his finger on the desktop. "The good news is, we find the guy behind the gun, and we solve two murders in one."

Nava smiled. "Shit, yeah."

"Don't get too excited. We got next to nothing." DeFore walked to Nava's desk and opened the folder. Inside was a single sheet. He pointed to it. "Gun isn't registered in any database we have. All we know is it's a rifle, and just about every house in the county has a hunting rifle. I bet there's more than there are people out here."

"Got that right."

"We're not gonna go door to door and do ballistics on every gun we find, so that's out."

"You'd get shot if you did that. These people and their second amendment and all that."

"It's their right. But that means we have a real intriguing clue, but no idea where it leads yet."

Nava steepled his fingers. "So what's the next move?"

"Let's go talk to the second vic's family. Justin didn't have anyone. Lived alone. Nobody at his job seems to know shit about him. But Chris has got a mother and a sister. Maybe they know something they didn't tell yet."

Nava checked his watch. DeFore knew why.

"Why don't you get on home to Maria. I can handle a simple door knock."

"You sure?"

"Yeah. Don't want to get you in hot water."

Nava had been married for over ten years. Twin girls six years old. DeFore had met his wife at a Fourth of July bar-b-que, and it was clear she ran the show at home. Not mean or overbearing, just a mama bear who liked things her way. And Nava was happy to be led on a leash.

DeFore's first instinct was to thank his stars he didn't have someone always over him, telling him where to be, how to behave, what to wear. But the more he thought about it, the older he got… man, he would love to have someone call the shots now and then. Someone to share a life with. Pick furniture, plan dinners, argue over the color of a new car. DeFore felt a pang of jealousy at every tiny annoyance in Nava's life.

"Okay," Nava said, already packing up. "I'll get the report in the morning."

"Yeah. Say hi to the family for me."

"Will do."

Nava stopped at the doorway. "We're gonna get this guy."

"No doubt about it."

Nava stepped out, leaving DeFore alone again.

Shit, shit, shit, shit, shit.

It didn't immediately look like a police car, but as Bree got closer, she saw the bubble light on the dashboard, the extra antennas on the trunk. Then she peeked inside and saw the radio and other junk that looked like it had been lifted right out of a black and white cruiser. She paced a tight circle in the street, wondering if she should get back in her car and drive. She stopped, took a deep breath. He'd been killed. Of course, there's gonna be questions. She just had to ride it out. Nothing to connect her to Chris's death. Nothing obvious, anyway.

"Breanna, where the hell you been?" Mama sat spilling over her chair. A cop in a suit jacket stood over her.

"I have a job, Mama. A life." She waved a hand over her Burger Barn uniform, pointing out the obvious.

The cop looked at her. He didn't wear a tie, no badge. She wondered for a second if he really was a cop. He held out his hand.

"Detective Brian DeFore. Sorry for your loss."

She shook his hand.

"Thanks. Did you catch who did it?"

"Uh, no, ma'am. The investigation is still ongoing."

His accent was pure parody, the kind actors go for to portray an upper Midwest rube. She wouldn't assume he was dumb, though.

"I was here, actually," DeFore said as Bree set down her purse. "To see if you could provide any information you didn't tell the officers you already spoke with."

"What are you, homicide?"

"Yes, ma'am."

Mama shifted in her seat and folded her arms across her chest as best she could. Her belly was so high, and her arms so thick they could barely meet in the middle. "I'm not telling this man shit about Christopher's personal life. That ain't none of his business."

"Mama, he's trying to find out who killed him."

"Doesn't mean we want all our dirty laundry hung out for everyone to see."

What do you know about laundry, Bree thought. She turned to the detective.

"You know he sold drugs, right?"

Mama nearly fell out of her chair. Would have if she wasn't so fused with it, the thing was nearly a part of her body. "Breanna!"

"We knew he had a record," DeFore said. He gave a short glance over his shoulder to Mama, then said, "Maybe you and I should talk in private."

Bree pointed to the front door. DeFore led the way, Mama complaining behind them.

"God, dammit, Breanna. Let the dead lie."

Bree followed DeFore to the front yard and shut the door on Mama's shouts behind them. They walked to the front of DeFore's car.

"So you think he was still selling?"

She scoffed. "I know he was. And you guys can't ever seem to arrest the people who push that shit."

"It's a difficult task."

"Easy as hell to buy it. You'd think it would be easier to catch people selling it."

"We get a dealer off the street, and he's gone for forty-eight hours before he pleas out or cops a deal. Vice is after the bigger fish."

"Yeah, Chris was a small fish, all right."

DeFore curled one side of his mouth into a wry smile. "Sounds like you and your brother didn't get along."

"You could say that."

"Do you know of anyone in particular who might want him dead?"

"You want an alphabetical list?"

He chuckled. "Breanna–"

"Bree."

"Bree. If you really do know something, you need to tell me now. I can see you don't share your mother's same feelings about his privacy."

"No, I don't. I'm sure Chris was gonna end up this way eventually. I know he worked for a guy named Dill. Other than that, I stayed out of his business, and he stayed out of mine."

DeFore nodded. "I know the name."

"Then go pick him up. There's your man."

"Was Christopher close with your neighbor, Justin Lyons?"

"They didn't even know each other. Unless Chris sold him shit, which is entirely possible."

"So they didn't hang out together?"

"Not that I saw."

Maybe she wasn't playing this right. Maybe she should steer suspicion toward her neighbor. This was coming at her fast, and it was all she could do to keep up.

"Kinda weird, two neighbors getting killed in the same week."

One of those non-questions meant to trip her up. She didn't bite.

"I guess."

DeFore watched her a while, then tapped his palm on his leg. "Well, if you do think of anything else, will you call me?" He handed her a business card. She took it.

"Sure."

"Pretty sure your Mom isn't calling any time soon."

"She doesn't like cops."

"So I see." He stepped around to the door of his unmarked car and gave her a small salute. "Thanks for your time, Bree."

She nodded at him, and as he drove off, she exhaled and wondered why she was always so damn scared to try out for drama club in high school. She was good at it.

The notes sounded good, his hands finding the chords quicker now, more easily. Carter strummed, and when he made a mistake, went back to the top and started over. The guitar rested on his good leg, his injured leg out to the side. He sat on the back porch and wondered how many nights music had been played out here on this very same guitar. The wood planks below him were well worn like the finish on the old guitar, like the callouses on his fingers from a lifetime of use.

A stiff, warm wind pushed the grass down almost flat in the back yard. Chester carved his way through in zig-zags, nose to the ground. The sun dipped below the horizon, and Carter stayed there until his coffee ran out, then gave a short whistle that made Chester's head pop up and turn back to him.

"Come on now, you're gonna get ticks out there."

Chester ignored him. Carter began the song again, this time adding in his voice. He didn't worry that his notes weren't as sweet as James Taylor's. He sounded better than the crows in the trees, and that's all that mattered. At the sound of his voice singing about a young cowboy who lived on the range, his horse and his cattle his only companions, Chester lifted his head from the grass. He came toward the music like it had a scent. Made Carter wonder if his old owner had sung out loud, too.

As Chester settled in beside him on the porch, bats darted overhead. He made it almost all the way through the song before he missed a chord and broke out laughing. Carter scratched Chester behind the ears.

"The way I see it," he said to Chester while looking out at the details of

156

the world fade away with the last of the light, "Every day ends in darkness. Night comes in whether we're ready or not. That's where I am. Sun has set, dark all around me. And that sun ain't gonna rise again. Not for me to see. So this is where I live now, in the darkness."

He let some time go by, thinking it over. Thinking how if he was going to live in the darkness, he might as well embrace it. He'd caused death. Can't take that back.

"But it's the natural way of it." He scratched more, thought more. "The ending of things is always in darkness."

As it always did, his thoughts were invaded by memories of Ava and Audrey. He smiled. The trees were only smudged shadows now, waiting for the moon to rise.

"Damn, though," he said. "We had some good days in the light."

He pushed off the post and limped toward the door, held the screen for Chester, who padded inside, then hitched up his bad leg over the threshold and went in.

Three days went by, and Carter had gotten used to his new hitching step. He limped from room to room and no longer needed to lean on things. He'd gone to spending his nights on the couch with Chester. The old dog didn't like the stairs, and Carter didn't care for them so much either since he'd been shot.

"Quite a pair," he said to Chester. "Bad hips, bad legs. At least I'm not as gassy as you are yet."

Chester barked once in agreement.

Carter had been feeling a low pain in his gut all day. The leg wound, and his prescription pills, had masked his other pains for a few days, but the leg wasn't hurting constantly anymore. Stiff and sore, but nothing an Advil couldn't help along. Now, his real pain had returned. He went to the kitchen and got his pill bottle off the counter. It was light, the rattle more hollow sounding. He undid the top and looked inside. Fewer than half remained. The doctor had given him three refills, but Carter had become a killer in his final days, and he'd be damned if he was going out an addict. He re-sealed the bottle and went back to the living room, gritting his teeth against the pain.

He grabbed a book on his way past the shelf. The newest Hap and Leonard book. He sat down, and when his body relaxed, the pain subsided enough for him to concentrate on the pages.

He'd gotten three chapters in, laughed out loud five times when Bree knocked on the door.

"Delivery," she said.

"C'mon in."

She pushed through, and Chester barked a few times until he recognized her; then he stood up quickly at the smell she brought in with her. She still wore her ugly brown and yellow uniform and carried a grease-stained bag from Burger Barn, which she held up and asked, "Who's hungry for lunch?"

Chester wove between her ankles as she tried to walk.

"I think you know the answer to that," Carter said.

Bree bent down and scratched at Chester with her free hand. "You're in luck, boy. Meat lover's special."

Bree unpacked the burgers, two sets of fries and an onion rings, and they set up the small table out on the back porch. She'd gotten Carter a double with cheese and grilled onions. A single for herself and three single patties, nothing but meat and cheese, for Chester.

"Good God, I'm in for an assault on my nose tonight."

Chester ate each burger in two chomps each and then sat beside the table and waited for more.

They ate in a quiet, casual way, like family, but both of them pretending they knew this was how families behave. Bree never knew the simple joy of family dinner, and Carter tried to avoid remembering because picturing Ava and Audrey in golden sunlight would only last until he remembered that they were both buried in cold ground beside one another, waiting for him to arrive soon.

"I'm going after that gun."

He wouldn't look at her when he spoke, wasn't even sure why he felt he needed to tell her. He dipped a fry in ketchup and chewed it.

"Be careful, okay?"

"I will."

She nodded her head at Chester, who stared at them with the focus of a chess player. "You taking him with you?"

"No. Might bark."

"I thought he had such a good nose."

"He does, but for things like this." He lifted his burger. Chester followed it with his eyes and licked the drool from his jowls.

"Well, those guys are nobody to fuck with."

"You know," Carter swallowed what was in his mouth, dabbed his lips with a napkin. "If my daughter said words like that to me at the table, I'd make her go wash her mouth out with soap."

Bree smiled around her mouthful of burger. "Different times, I guess."

Carter slapped a mosquito on his neck, checked the smear of blood on his palm. "There's one thing I won't miss at all."

He hadn't realized he'd said it, or what it really meant until he saw the stricken look on Bree's face. Again, he turned his eyes away from hers.

"So is it, like, painful?"

"Sometimes," he said. "Doctor gave me pills, but I don't like taking too many."

"And there's nothing they can do?"

Carter shook his head. "Hundred percent fatality, he said. I told him life has a hundred percent fatality rate. Only difference is I got an expiration date on mine."

Bree looked on the verge of tears.

"Aw, hell," he said. "My troubles are the last thing you should put your mind to. You got plans to make. California, right?"

His attempt to change the subject failed.

"You're a good man, Carter. You know that, right?"

He leaned back in his chair and chuckled. "Well, I made it seventy-two years before I killed anybody. I only wish I'd known sooner the bar for goodness was so low. I'd have worried a lot less." He tossed the last hunk of his burger to Chester, who caught it out of the air.

"You know what I mean," Bree said. "You did me a big favor. You loved your wife and your daughter. You never ran out on them, and if you ever cheated, I don't want to know about it." She pointed at Chester. "Look at the way he looks at you. Dogs know good people."

"Dogs know the one that feeds them."

She pushed her plate away from her and crossed her arms. "Jesus, just take a fucking compliment."

He let her stew for a moment, then sighed. "Look, Bree, thanks. But you have to understand I don't feel like such a good person right now. I've done bad things, and I know they're bad. I had my reasons, but that doesn't make them right."

Another mosquito buzzed past his ear. Bree looked out over the back yard.

"Thanks for lunch," he said. "I gotta get going if I want to find that gun."

Bree stood. "Will you promise me to be careful?"

Carter nodded. Bree reached in her pocket and took out her knife. "At least take this. It's something."

"I won't need that."

She held it out and didn't move. "Take it."

Carter took it from her and put it in his own pocket. "I'll be fine."

"Your leg says otherwise, old man."

Detective Brian DeFore yawned and then stretched. He stood from his desk, where he'd been watching traffic cameras for hours, and walked to the other side of the room to refill his coffee. He added two creamers and two sugars and took a sip while standing, not eager to get back to making notes on cars driving past the crime scenes. He'd requested the three days prior and one day after the killings. His only solace was that this was far from the big city where there might be a camera on every corner. He had three, and each one was more than three blocks from where Justin and Christopher lived and miles from where Christopher's body was found.

So far, he had three pages of notes: white Ford, license 3FY, 2 pm. Writing out the full license was too much work, he decided. And full make and model, too. He needed a shorthand. If anything hit with those small details, he'd go back and re-check. So far, a whole lot of nothing except proof positive that people in this county liked their trucks and SUVs. In all the footage he watched, he saw no electric cars and only one hybrid. Must be out-of-towners.

Chief Winters filled the doorway and knocked on the jamb. DeFore knew if he was knocking, it couldn't be a good visit.

"How's it coming, Brian?"

DeFore let out a deep exhale. "Slowly. I won't bullshit you."

"I appreciate that."

"Got some stuff cooking, though. New angles."

"I'm staying out of your hair."

DeFore nodded once in acknowledgment and appreciation.

"Thing is," Chief Winters continued, "All eyes are on this. With so few cases across your desk and now two at once. People are paying attention, is all I'm saying."

"I know they are." DeFore tried to read the Chief's face. "You telling me the clock is ticking?"

"I'm not telling you. But if you listen close…"

"I get you."

Chief Winters knocked twice on the door jamb again to punctuate the end of the conversation, dipped his chin to say goodbye, and was gone, leaving DeFore to wonder how much time he had left on this case before they brought in someone from one of the cities to take over.

Nava came in, shaking rain off his coat.

"Hey."

"Hey there."

Nava sat, and DeFore slowly made his way back to his desk to pull up the next file on his screen.

"Get anything?" DeFore asked.

"Christopher was well known on the streets. Dealt meth, coke, pot. Could get heroin if you asked but didn't carry, it looks like."

"Why is it we can know so much about these guys, and we can't ever seem to bust them?"

Nava raised both hands like he was being held up. "Preaching to the choir, man."

"Y'know, that girl, the sister, she asked me why we didn't bust Dill. I had no fucking answer for her other than the system sucks sometimes."

"Takes time."

"Yeah. Maybe our perp has the right idea."

"Take 'em out with a hunting rifle?"

DeFore took another sip and waved Nava away. Just cop talk. They had to say it out loud now and then, so nobody went off and did something crazy. Two, three, ten times, you get a case thrown out or somebody pleas down to nothing, and a little frontier justice starts to look good to you.

"You get anywhere with that?" Nava asked, lifting his chin toward the computer screen.

DeFore shrugged. "No. I saw the girl's brown Civic twice and Christopher's car twice, both at night. But that doesn't do me any good."

Nava ran a hand through his hair, wiping away any lingering rainwater. "You think she could have had something to do with it? You said there was no love lost there, right?"

"I mean, never say never. But I don't see it."

Nava opened the top desk drawer, took out a roll of mints, thumbed one out, and put it in his mouth. "Maybe you just want to keep this case going to give you something to do. Only May, and you've already caught your case of the year." He held out the mints to DeFore, who waved him off.

"People ask what's real detective work?" He pointed to his screen. "It's this shit."

"Again, preaching to the choir."

Carter regretted not taking another pill. He rolled past the turnoff and went another half mile down the two-lane to make sure nobody else was around. An area like this, between farms, he could go hours without seeing anyone else. He had to give it to the drug dealers; they picked a great place for their headquarters.

He angled his truck off the road but didn't make it very far down the path into the trees where the trailers were. He pulled off and tried to get himself behind a tree so he couldn't see the highway, and hopefully no one could see him.

Carter got out and took a moment with his hand on the door handle, breathing deep and letting a wave of pain pass by. The day was warm, and the sun cooked the soil in the fields all around them, filling the air with a loamy scent of dry manure and budding plants.

He walked the path, staying off in a ditch to the side, looking for any sign of where his shootout with Chris took place. He stopped when he got his first glimpse of the trailers through the trees. He crouched low and started searching the ground. Dead leaves covered the ground an inch thick. He toed through them in his boots like they were snow drifts, kicking aside piles of dry, brown leaves searching for the gun. It didn't help that the stock of the rifle was a honey-colored wood, easy camouflage for this ground cover.

Carter knew the gun would be on the right side of the driveway. He'd been on the right side of his truck and had spun that way when he lost his grip. Being here, he could still hear the echoes of the gunshots in the branches. The blood on Chris's chest had been so red in the harsh light of his headlamps. He'd fallen so unlike someone who had tripped or taken a spill Carter had ever seen. Chris's body moved like he was being pulled to the ground, his arms and legs not stiff and resistant to the fall like someone would be if they were trying to protect themselves.

The static sound of dry leaves was steady as he made small circles in his search. He didn't notice many birds or insect noises. He thought how much Chester would love to get his nose in here and root around.

He noticed the black line of the barrel as much for the fact that it was straight when nothing else out here was. The gun sat on top of the leaves, the wood blending in perfectly with the ground. Before he bent to pick it up, he turned and looked at the flat ground of the road, only fifteen feet to his left. The ruts and gouges of his truck tires and Chris's car tires were still there. He expected he might see a blood stain, but saw only dirt. He looked up to see how close he'd gotten to the trailers. He could see three of them clearly now, a fourth hidden behind the trio. A large propane tank the size of a car sat up against one trailer, and he could see a small port on the roof releasing steam or smoke into the air. He saw two cars parked in the clearing.

He kept low and tried to move fast back to his truck, hitching his lame leg along behind him. He got in and wiped his sleeve across his forehead to clear away sweat. His didn't notice the pain at all, adrenaline had taken care of that. The shells were still in his glove box. He didn't like his next thought.

Chris was gone, but the trailers were still making the drugs. Someone was still out there selling to kids. Kids like Katy, Bree's friend. They obviously needed that propane to cook the stuff. Maybe he could throw a little wrench into their works. Disrupt the manufacturing. It wasn't much, but it felt wrong to be right here and just let it go on unimpeded. Like doing nothing was some sort of unspoken endorsement.

Carter loaded a shell. He moved between the trees back to where he could see the trailer with the tank clearly. It was a big enough target he felt good being this far away. Maybe they wouldn't hear the shot, even. The gas would run out, and they wouldn't know why, then when they checked it, they'd see the leak. Yes, they'd replace it, but for a few days, the supply would be cut off. Maybe it would be enough for some kid to get help.

He sighted the side of the white tank. Hunting with his dad, he never took a shot at anything bigger than a rabbit. If everything he hunted were this big and this immobile, he'd have had a much better success rate.

Holding still, he felt the pain in his leg grow and radiate through his body. He knew he'd be feeling this extra trip into the woods on the ride home. When he got back, he'd tip a pill out of the bottle and lay on the couch with Chester.

Carter squeezed the trigger and felt the rifle kick into his shoulder. He heard the clank of the shell hitting the tank like banging on a pan with a metal spoon. A split second later, a short geyser of flame shot straight up. Carter jolted, he turned first one direction and then another. He hadn't expected that.

"Goddamn it, no."

He broke into a limping run back toward his truck when there was a bigger bang behind him. He turned and saw half the trailer in flames now. He kept low, zig-zagging and trying to run forward while looking behind him. His leg kept him from moving in anything other than a repeated fall forward, then catching himself just before he landed flat on his face. He saw two people jump out of the trailer and rip off face masks as they ran to put distance between them and the bomb on the side of the trailer.

Carter stopped looking and limped for the truck as fast as he could. He wheezed with burning lungs by the time he reached the driver's door.

"You dumb-ass son of a bitch," he said as he climbed inside, wishing Chester was there with him so he had someone to talk to about how stupid he was. He threw the rifle into the passenger seat and made an awkward four-point turn in the dirt before gunning the engine back out onto the two-lane.

Dill watched the bed of a red truck bounce onto the highway. It was too far to read the plate, but he wasn't worried. The new camera he'd installed would do that for him.

A skinny guy named Waco ran up to him.

"The fuck was that?"

Dill lifted his chin in the direction he was looking. "We had a visitor."

"Well, fuck, let's go." Waco made a step toward the cars, but Dill halted him.

"Hold up." Waco froze. "We won't catch him on the road. Go check the monitor. I know a guy who can get us info from the plates."

"If he didn't steal the car."

"Would you steal a piece of shit pickup truck?"

Dill turned toward his burning trailer, two doors down from his office.

"What do we do?" Waco asked.

"Let it burn out. Too hot to get in there to the shut-off valve. And we think real hard about who might want to do this to us."

The two lab workers huddled together near the cars, coughing and clinging to each other. Dill ground his teeth as he watched the trailer burn.

"I got some ideas."

"Shit, man," Waco said. "First, they take out C-Money, and now this. It's fucking war, man."

The flames shot straight up, a single finger of red-orange fire. They were clear of the trees enough he didn't think it would catch and cause a bigger problem. It did mean a break in the cook. That meant a delay. That meant money. Might as well steal cash from his pocket.

"Y'know, if it weren't mine," Dill said. "It'd be fucking beautiful."

One of the tires on the trailer popped in the heat, and the whole structure tipped to the right. Dill turned away and went inside his own trailer to check the camera. Too bad it had taken Chris getting shot for him to install it.

The smell reached DeFore before the door even opened. Nava brought tacos.

"Hey," he said through a mouthful of chips.

"Jesus, man, at least wait until you sit down."

Nava was shamed like a child. "I was hungry."

DeFore pointed toward Nava's gut. "You're hungry a lot these days."

Nava sat. "Yeah, okay, I'm not the same as when I walked a beat, but my doctor says I'm healthy."

"Yeah, well, your waistline says you like ice cream."

The extra work on the twin murder cases meant Nava had an excuse to ignore his wife's diet restrictions. DeFore worked decently hard to keep in shape in case he ever pulled the trigger and got back in the dating pool. Age and the savory smell of those tacos weren't helping, though.

DeFore stood and ran a hand down his face, exhaling. He opened the bag and took out his two tacos and some chips, put them on a napkin he spread on Nava's desk, keeping his own clean.

"You find anything yet?" Nava asked.

Four more hours of scrolling and scanning the traffic camera. The police work you don't see on TV.

"I got one thing: a red truck. It passed by a little before and after time of death on Justin and was on the same camera the same day Christopher went missing. Not much, but I figure I'll check on it if it gets me out of this chair for an hour."

Nava took his time to chew and swallow what was clearly too large of

170

a bite. He sucked some Diet Coke through a straw and set down his taco. "You ever think we're spending too much time on this?" he asked. "I mean, shit, do these scumbags even deserve this much effort?"

"Damn, son. You're a half hour late on lunch, and you get in a mood."

"Come on, you know what I'm saying."

DeFore dipped a chip in some guacamole. "Yeah, I know. If I thought it was just a drug thing or if it was gonna stay with just these jerks, maybe. But I still don't know the connection, and it could mean someone is doing something random. What if someone else on the same block gets shot next?"

"Some serial killer targeting one block?"

"Don't underestimate the crazy people are capable of."

"Oh, I don't." Nava took another too-large bite.

"Besides," DeFore said. "I've been thinking, what if this traces back to Dill or someone higher? What if Christopher pissed someone off? Maybe we can pin this to someone really worth getting."

"Like getting Capone on tax fraud. You get the bad guy on something other than what they're known for."

DeFore gave a nod and a head tilt. "Sort of like that. But if we can nail someone for murder that they can't plea out of or hide behind some other bullshit, and it gets another scumbag off the street? Then why not keep working this? We got two assholes off the street, and we can get one more as a bonus."

"Like getting fouled and still making the basket, then you get a free throw too."

DeFore shook his head. "Just eat your tacos, man."

Nava obliged and took another huge bite. One taco down, two more to go. A quick knock at the open door was followed by a uniformed officer stepping in with a sheet of paper held out before her. "Got your I.D., Detective."

DeFore was chewing, so he didn't speak but waved his hand for her to come over. She handed off the piece of paper as he swallowed. "Thanks."

"Anything else? Gotta say I wish I was working this case with you guys. More exciting than what usually walks in the front door."

DeFore hooked a thumb over at Nava. "Well, when this one croaks of a heart attack from clogged arteries, you're my first call."

"I'll hold you to that." The officer smiled and gave a small wave as she walked out the door.

"That your red truck?" Nava asked.

"Yep." DeFore read the page. "Carter McCoy." He read down the page further and frowned. "Age seventy-two." He let the page fall to his desk, discarded. He tucked into his second taco, un-rushed to get to an old man's house to ask him about murder.

Nava had turned serious. "What's that name again? McCoy?"

"Yeah."

Nava wiped his hands quickly on a wad of paper napkins and began rifling through pages on his desk. Near the bottom of a pile, he came up with what he was looking for. "Here. Yeah, I thought that sounded familiar."

"What?"

"The girl Justin Lyons went to prison for killing was named Audrey McCoy." He looked up from his file and met DeFore's eye. "Father's name, Carter McCoy."

"You don't say."

DeFore picked up the one sheet again. He was done with lunch. He had an old man to see.

Bree crept into the house and eased the screen door shut behind her. Not the usual slap of wood on wood she usually let happen. Didn't want to wake Mama.

She brought with her the stink of french fry grease and burnt beef patties. It clung to every fiber of her polyester uniform, and no amount of washing would get rid of it. She knew she'd be sweating out the stench from her pores until she stood on a beach in California and let the sea breeze blow it away.

But Mama wasn't asleep in her chair. She sat at the kitchen table, eyes red and wet, a bottle of Vodka open in front of her. Bree's attention had been in the wrong direction, and Mama surprised her when she spoke.

"Breanna."

Bree stopped where she was, but didn't know what to say to Mama.

"Lookit you out there, working a job, keeping on. You always were the good one."

Bree didn't know how to react to what sounded like a compliment. That brand of communicating came so rare from Mama, she figured it was sarcasm. Then she saw the bottle and gave credit for anything nice Mama had to say to the eighty-proof inside. But Mama looked at her with a softness she hadn't in years. The drink slurred her voice a little, but the words sounded rehearsed, like she'd been sitting here alone and thinking them before they came out.

"Goddamn, your brother was...I know what he was. But he was a good boy. Inside there, he was good. He just needed to get beyond this part. All this Cash Money bullshit. He needed to find himself." She tilted her head and looked at Bree like she was a tiny kitten. "But you…my girl. My sweet girl. So good. So smart. So pretty, even with your father's red hair." She clung two-handed to the bottle.

"Mama, I–"

"You're all I got now." Tears rolled from her eyes, probably fifty percent vodka.

"That's not true."

Mama let out a single snort of a laugh. She waved her hand around the room, the long droop of fat from her arm wobbling in the air. "You mean this? Or you mean, what? All my gentleman callers?"

The meanness had started creeping back into her voice.

"You can't just sit here and expect it all to come to you," Bree said. "You want your life to be better, you gotta go do something about it."

Mama gripped the neck of the vodka bottle in her chubby hand. She wept now, her words coming in high-pitched tones. "I know, I know, I know. I'm fucking useless. I ruined everything. I pushed everyone away. It's the men, Breanna. They'll ruin everything for you. Men are evil. They knock you up and leave. They push you around and expect you to take it."

Bree took a step toward the hallway. "Mama, I think you need some rest."

"I do, I do. I need to rest. My god, I haven't had a decent sleep in years."

She lifted the bottle to her lips and drank. Bree sighed, let her shoulders slump.

"Come on, Mama. Let's get you to bed."

She went to her mother, pried the bottle from her hand. Mama seemed confused by her attention. Bree couldn't recall the last time she'd touched her mother. She tugged on her arm.

"C'mon. Stand up."

Mama pushed back from the table, pressed both hands down on the top, and pushed herself up. She swayed, and Bree had to brace herself against the cabinets to hold her up. Mama set a sweaty hand against Bree's bright hair and stroked her like she was smearing mud.

"So good. Such a good girl."

174

"Okay, Mama." She knew this version of Mama would be gone by morning when she sobered up. She tugged at her again and got her moving toward the hall.

"They took my baby boy," Mama said. "They took him from me."

"Come on, let's go. Almost there."

Mama shuffle-stepped, leaned on Bree like a crutch.

"Every man in your life will leave you," she said. "Every last one of them. Even your own son."

Bree hadn't had enough men in her life to corroborate this. She urged her mother down the hall and guided her through her bedroom door. Mama's queen-sized stood unmade, the sheets in a tangle like there'd been a fight there even though it had been weeks, if not months, since Mama had slept here and not in her chair. Bree got Mama to pivot and sat her down on the edge of the bed.

"Okay, there you go. You got it?"

Mama sat there, panting like a dog in the sun. She stared at the carpet, but her mind was miles away. Lost in memory and regrets. A place Bree never wanted to live. A place Bree was determined to pack up and drive away from. Mama would feel this same sadness, maybe worse, with both her kids gone. But that wasn't Bree's problem. If this woman refused to do anything to help herself, she wasn't going to drag Bree down with her.

Still, her hand lingered on Mama's arm until she felt she was stable on the bed and wouldn't slide off onto the floor. She could look at her mother's eyes now that they were focused somewhere far away. She could try to see them without feeling her judgmental stare back at her. She knew there was a life somewhere in the past where Mama had the same dreams and plans. A life when she was beautiful, she was young, when she had a long road stretched before her. She knew much of Mama's sadness was that she could see it too in every mirror, every memory, every movement of her children, who were what she once was and would never be again. Bree knew that must be sad. Must break her heart every day.

"You gonna be okay, Mama?"

Mama nodded, eyes still glazed.

175

"You lay down now and sleep."

"You're my baby girl, Breanna." Mama's words were a slush, fighting around a heavy tongue. "I love you, baby girl."

Bree took a step back. The words made her recoil from the unfamiliarity. She wanted Mama to say it again so she could be sure she hadn't misheard, but "Baby" was all she repeated.

She stood back, and Mama hoisted her legs onto the mattress. They hung near the edge, but Bree felt sure she wouldn't tumble out of bed. Mama's eyes closed, and almost immediately, her breathing turned heavy, on the verge of a snore.

Bree stood in the doorway and watched Mama sleep. She'd given Bree life, raised her, and, in her own way, given her the lessons she needed from life. Examples of what not to be, what not to do. There was no string that tied them together. Mama had let Bree go years ago. Dropped her to float in the air and find her own footing like a cat falling from a tree. But she would land on all fours; she would walk away and live nine more lives.

She went down the hall to her room to peel off her uniform. First, a shower, and then she would count her money again, then go see Katy. Maybe they had enough. Maybe they could make it.

Chris's room was still closed. The police had looked in there, but hadn't torn it apart in a search, as far as she knew. Chris would have money. He always had stashes. Maybe the cops found it, but maybe they didn't.

Bree turned and walked across the hall, and opened Chris's door. The room smelled of stale pot smoke and sweat. There was dirty laundry on the floor a pile of mismatched sneakers in the corner of the room. His laptop was gone, either the cops took it or Mama had sold it already.

She turned over the mattress first. Nothing underneath. He had no bed frame, just a boxspring on the floor. She lifted one corner and tried seeing under. It was too heavy to hold for long. She propped up one corner with a pair of shoes and took out her phone to shine the flashlight under. No money there.

She opened all the dresser drawers, looked under each drawer for a taped bundle. In his closet, she searched the top shelf but found only old yearbooks, a stack of comics, more dirty clothes, and a pair of broken speakers. She turned out all the pockets of his pants and hoodies and jackets and came up with twenty-three dollars. If there was something else here, she couldn't find it. Thanks again for nothing, Christopher.

It had been an hour since Carter came inside, cursing himself.

"Dumb son of a bitch. Crazy old man. How could you be so stupid?"

Chester sensed his anxiety and hadn't settled since he came in, the most Carter had seen him up and about since he brought him home. Carter set the gun propped against the armchair. He knew he needed a pain pill, but didn't want to take one. He wasn't sure if the pain was exacerbated by the stress, or if it was merely the disease reminding him of the ticking clock.

The pain in his leg, his gut, the pounding in his head. He sat on the couch and looked at the gun and thought there might be another way out of this.

He ignored Chester, circling his legs as he loaded a fresh round into the rifle. He sat down on the couch and set the butt of the gun on the floor, the long barrel now aimed up to where he sat. He leaned over until the empty circle started back at him. He weighed the pros and cons. End the pain, or go on until his body gave out? Accept the inevitable, or keep moving until the last ounce of energy was drained? Finish reading that damn book, or let it go.

He had to reach down to the full extent of his arm to lay a finger on the trigger. He could get the barrel up under his chin if he leaned out and stretched his neck like a turtle peering out of its shell.

Chester made a high-pitched noise in the back of his throat like he knew something was wrong. He sat next to Carter, hot breath on his leg right above the wound. Carter turned his eyes to the dog. The red-veined eyes looked back, and he licked his chops. If Carter pulled that trigger, Chester would be alone. He'd already been through that once before. No, Carter couldn't do that to him.

He let go of the gun and let it fall to the floor in front of the couch. The stock blended in with the floorboards, the barrel poked under the couch skirt. Chester licked his jowls again.

"Okay, you win." Carter stood and petted the dog on the head. "Dinner for you, a pill for me."

Chester followed him into the kitchen.

Dill and Waco had been watching the house for nearly an hour. One phone call, and Dill had the old man's address from his license plate. The frightened cop on the other end of the line gave him the info and tried to plead, "We're even now, okay? No more of this bullshit."

"Sure, sure," Dill lied. Once you had a cop by the balls, you had him for life, and you never let go, only squeezed harder.

The isolated farmhouse wasn't anyplace Dill knew about. There were no other cars around, no security he could see. Looked like the house of an old man who lived alone. But how could that be?

"There's nobody else here, I'm telling you," Waco said.

"There's gotta be. You think some crazy old man drove by and just decided to shoot up our trailers?"

"Maybe he was hunting and missed."

"Hunting out there?"

"A lotta guys see a deer while they're driving and pull up to take a shot at it. Like, they don't even get out of the car."

Dill shook his head, eyes still on the house. "I dunno."

He didn't know of any crews that hired old guys. Didn't know anyone who was particularly pissed off at him right now. This was an unprovoked attack, and he didn't see any way it wasn't related to C-Money getting killed. *That* he could picture—that dipshit pissing someone off, starting a war without even knowing it.

"I bet the truck was stolen," Waco said. "Not even the old man driving it."

"Sure looked like it from the video."

"Maybe he's in disguise?"

Dill shot him a look that told him how dumb he thought that idea was.

"So he steals a truck, disguises himself as the driver, then drives back to the old guy's house and just hangs out?"

"Shit, Dill, I dunno. Let's go knock on the fucking door and find out."

This waiting was boring. Yeah, it was time to move. Dill didn't say Waco was right, just opened the door to the car and got out. Let Waco chase him like a puppy following his master,

The walk up the lane to the house was slow going, with their sneakers slipping in the tire ruts. Dill's head swiveled back and forth, looking for some security measure he hadn't spotted yet. He saw nothing but an overgrown yard and a rusty lawnmower.

They stepped up to the porch, scanning for eyes, watching them from windows or cameras hidden in corners. Seeing nothing, Dill knocked.

He looked at the book on the coffee table, wondering if reading would help calm him. He knew he wouldn't be able to focus, though. That damn book might go unread, and he'd never know the ending.

"Ain't that life, though?" he said to Chester. The dog finally settled on the rug next to him, seeming to know Carter needed a little extra space on the couch to stretch out. Chester's elevated stress levels hadn't done any good for his gas. Once he laid down and let out a long snorting exhale, he also expelled a cloud of noxious stench that Carter was too tired to do anything about other than scold him, "Oh, sweet Jesus, Chester."

It prompted Carter to get up. His leg was feeling better when he stayed still. The pain of the hole through his flesh had diminished, but when he put any weight on it, the reminder that he'd been shot was still there. But weight was all he had. He'd taken on a lot more to carry in the past few days. Might be his leg now, but his back was sure to buckle soon under it all.

He carried his guitar back to the couch. He took a long moment, getting himself settled so his leg calmed down. He strummed a while, putting together familiar chords in familiar patterns. The same building blocks of a million songs. Only difference was the words.

He assumed the knock was Bree. Knuckles sounded like knuckles in three short raps, no matter whose. No smell of beef fat and fry grease preceded her this time, but he had no other visitors these days. The pain pill hadn't taken hold quite yet, but the edges were worn down.

"Come in."

The door opened a few inches, but nobody appeared. Not the usual storm of an entrance Bree used. Chester looked up from the floor, on alert. Two faces appeared. Men. One with a shaved head and one a foot taller and with a face that looked like it was made out of clay. The shaved-headed one stepped in first.

"You McCoy?"

"Who're you?" Carter set the guitar aside, slid the pick between the strings to hold it.

"Anyone else here?"

The bigger one peeked in corners and around doorways in a slow search.

"Who are you? This is my house."

"My name's Dill. I'm the one whose propane tank you blew all to shit."

Carter felt a spasm clench his stomach. Chester stood halfway on his front paws only, keeping the two men in sight and grumbling in the back of his throat.

The big one came back from down the hall. "Nobody else here that I can see."

Dill laughed. "I gotta be honest with you, McCoy. I expected a whole crew up in here. And all I got is one old man?"

"I don't know what you're talking about, propane tank."

Dill's expression turned hard. "Let's not start with the bullshit." His arms were tangled with tattoos, his jeans, two sizes too big. The big one joined him at his side. "I haven't even brought up what you did to C-Money."

Carter knew right then this was where it ended. He should have pulled that trigger an hour ago, done it on his own terms. Now some drug dealing punk was going to kill him in his own house with his dog watching.

"What do we do about this?" Dill said.

"What do you mean?"

"You blew my shit up, man. Someone pay you to do that?"

"No."

"What about the hit on C-Money?"

"It was no hit."

The two men formed a small wall between Carter and the front door. Chester hadn't stopped the low growl in his chest, but he stayed planted on the floor in front of Carter.

"So, who you workin' for?"

Carter couldn't tell if this guy, this Dill, was trying to get to Bree or not. "Nobody."

"So what gives, man? Why you targeting my shit?"

"Me and Chris, that was something else. Just between him and me."

"He sell to your grandkids or something?"

"That's between him and me."

"Well, he ain't around, so I can't get it out of him."

"Look." Carter moved to stand up, but the big one put a hand out, and Carter stayed where he was. Chester's growl grew a little louder.

"Look," Carter said again. "I'm sorry. It was an accident."

Dill smiled. "Nah, nah, man. This is an accident."

He kicked out with his right leg and knocked the reading lamp off the little side table next to the armchair. The table spun and fell to the floor; the lamp hit the hardwood and burst into pieces. The box of rifle shells had been opened and scattered on the floor with tiny metal chimes. Chester stood on all fours and barked. Carter hooked his hand in the dog's collar and held him firm. The big one pulled a gun from his waistband and pointed it at Chester.

"Tell him to shut it, old man."

"Chester, quiet." Carter's words had no effect.

Dill was mad now. His voice raised over Chester's barking. "Nobody comes to my house and pulls that shit, man. Not without paying. So let's see what you got to bargain with."

"Nothing. I have nothing."

"You better hope you can find something, man. 'Cause no matter what— you got blood, and I take that as payment."

"Okay, okay." Carter put his one arm out, pleading, the other still holding Chester. He was frail, old. Defeated, and he knew it. He thought about letting it happen. Let the punk kill him. All he'd be doing is turning the clock forward a few weeks. He had a feeling it wouldn't go quickly, though. And there was nothing here he needed to keep. Let the bastard take it all.

"The guitar. This guitar. Worth a lot of money." He pointed to it propped against the couch cushion next to him.

Dill and his partner traded a look. "This thing? Shit, that's ancient, man."

The big one moved to grab it, and Chester barked louder, aiming it at him. The man straightened and pointed the gun again. "Yo, tell him to shut the fuck up."

"Chester, quiet. Stop it."

Carter tugged on his collar, and Chester calmed for a moment, enough to let the man reach across and lift the guitar. He spun it by the neck, turning it over a few times in his hand.

"What'd you think, Waco?"

"Ah, it ain't shit, man. It's old as fuck."

Carter held out a pleading hand. "No, no, no. That's why it's valuable. Thousands. That's what they told me."

"A dusty old guitar?"

"Yes. Honestly."

"Fuck that, man."

Waco let it fall roughly into the armchair. The strings let out a tuneless clang.

"Gotta do better than that, old man," Dill said. He stepped to the bookshelf and pointed at the photo of Ava. "Where's your wife at? She got jewelry or shit?"

"My wife passed away."

"So she won't miss shit."

"She didn't have any jewelry. We made a modest living."

Chester watched Dill walk back to his place between the couch and the door. The hair on his back stood in a ridge across his spine.

"Looks like you don't have shit," Dill said.

"What do you want from me?"

"Money, bitch." Dill kicked at the fallen side table. "You blew up my shit."

Chester set off a fury of barking again. Waco threatened with the gun. "Yo, tell that bitch to shut the fuck up."

Carter pushed his body to the edge of the couch, putting himself between

185

the gun and the dog. He tried telling Chester to be quiet, but the dog knew this was all wrong. Knew this was trouble.

"Look, kill me if you have to. Leave the dog alone."

"You giving up, old man?" Dill said. "That's it? Just kill me?"

"I don't have what you're looking for, and I don't have the time to explain everything. You came here to kill me, so do it."

"I came here to get paid."

"Then take the guitar. If not, go ahead and shoot me."

Carter felt the rifle against his heel. It was pushed halfway under the couch. He hadn't moved it from where it had fallen when he brought it back home. He knew the barrel probably still smelled from the shot at Dill's propane tank. He also knew there was one more round loaded that he never got to fire.

Dill grinned and said to Waco, "I can't tell if this old man is brave as shit or dumb as shit."

"I say dumb as shit." He stepped forward and racked the slide on his gun like he'd been practicing in a mirror at home. "I'm gonna shut that fuckin' dog up right now, though."

Carter knew what his life was worth. That he'd put himself in this situation. But Chester hadn't done a damn thing. Carter bent and lifted the rifle from where it lay at his feet. They hadn't even seen it there. He came up with the barrel pointing out, and he squeezed. The rifle jumped in his hands, too low to brace it against anything. In the muzzle flash, he saw images of Justin's face go slack, and he saw Chris feel the impact of his bullet.

Waco jerked back as if punched. He dropped his pistol.

Dill lost all the confidence in his posture as he watched Waco fall to the floor. Chester, jolted by the blast, leapt forward and charged Dill. He clamped down on his right wrist and brought Dill to the ground.

Carter pushed himself up off the couch and wavered on his one good leg for a moment. Waco was moving slightly, but all efforts were focused on his belly, where he seemed to claw at the wound, trying to dig the shell out with his fingers.

Dill lunged forward with his left hand and placed it over the fallen pistol.

Chester hadn't let go of his wrist. Dill turned and aimed the gun at the crown of Chester's skull.

Carter swung the rifle around and hit Dill in the side of the head with the stock. He fell to the floor again, dropping the pistol. Chester growled and kept a firm clamp on Dill's wrist.

Carter dropped to his knees and felt around the floor for one of the fallen shells. He couldn't bend his bad leg and had to lean on one elbow to reach under the couch. He came out with a dull brass shell. Carter loaded it into the gun and looked up to see Dill bringing the pistol back around to Chester's head. He moved his arm along with the swinging of the dog's neck. Dill didn't want to blast his own hand off, and Chester jerked his head side to side in quick, unpredictable movements. Blood started to flow from Dill's wrist.

Carter pushed himself up, and with a deep yell, he forced his bad leg under him to bear weight. He pushed the gun forward, braced it against his shoulder, and set the barrel inches from Dill's mouth. Carter didn't plead with the man, didn't bargain with him. He shot.

The sound made Chester release, and Dill fell back, dead.

Carter dropped the gun, put an arm around the dog, and held him close. "It's okay, boy. It's okay."

Chester breathed hard into Carter's embrace. Waco had gone still. The house smelled of blood and rifle shots. But a quiet descended on them. Carter held the dog to him and sat watching the still bodies, waiting for the ringing in his ears to subside.

Every time she got behind the wheel, she thought, *Go. Now. Just go*.

She drove to Katy's, thinking the money didn't matter anymore. When would it ever be enough? She wanted to see what Katy had left over and figure a way to make it work. In the time it would take them to pack, they could be gone. Her asshole dad would be left in the dust, and Bree's Mama could cry in the dark until her heart gave out.

She felt the strongest pull from Carter. The old man was still recovering from the gunshot he'd sustained while doing her murder-for-hire. But he'd be fine. Tough old dude, and he had a great dog with him. No much you can't do with a great dog by your side. Plus, he was dying anyway. She felt awful for thinking it. Sounded dismissive, but it was true. Should she keep her life on hold, waiting for him to kick off?

In the short time she knew Carter, she knew he wouldn't want that.

She parked at Katy's feeling nervous energy, a static crackle like rubbing flat-footed over carpet and touching a doorknob. She bypassed the front door and went around the side to Katy's room. She heard the low bellow of Katy's dad and could tell he was in rare form, maybe drunk. Katy's mom would be at work. Again. Always.

Bree stood under the window, crouched down so she couldn't be seen, but the sound came through like a loud TV in a motel room next door. The first thing she heard was the familiar sound of Katy's tears.

"What kind of fuck up are you gonna let your life become?" he asked. "How long have you been on this shit? Huh?"

He'd found her drugs. The shit Chris had sold her. Bree hated to think

188

she already had a new dealer. It meant the money might be all gone.

"I mean, I knew you were stupid, but not this stupid."

Katy had no answer, only tears and sobs of anguish. Bree felt her muscles tense, her face flush. She could hear him ripping through her room. Things hitting the floor, drawers torn open.

"Is this all of it? Huh?"

He'd say his anger was only protecting his child. Keeping her off the glass pipe was a father's duty. But his way of doing things always ended in tears and a red welt on the side of Katy's face. Bree could only assume that had already happened before she got there. The minute he found the pipe, or the bag of rocks.

"You're gonna tell me who sold you this shit."

"No, Daddy."

She sounded so small. So fragile. He sounded like the giant in a fairy tale.

"You damn well are too. Who is it?"

"I'm done. That's old. I haven't done it in a while. I'm all done."

"How could you be so fucking stupid in the first place?"

Something heavy hit the floor. Katy's cries rose in pitch and volume.

"What's this?"

Bree wanted to look, but she knew if he saw her, it would be bad for both girls.

"How much is here?"

"Daddy, no."

"Is this your drug money? Are you stealing from me?"

Bree felt her hands go cold. He'd found her money. *Their* money. Escape money.

"No, Daddy."

"Then where did you get it? You don't make this much. Are you selling drugs, too?"

Bree heard the slap. It made her flinch, and she felt a hot pain on her cheek, but she knew it was nothing like what Katy was feeling.

"What are you selling then? Your body, you little slut?"

Another slap and Katy screamed, "No."

"This is mine now."

This was as bad as Bree had ever heard it. She couldn't cower under a window anymore. She stood, walked to the front of the house, and went in the door.

She stopped in the doorway to Katy's room and saw her father standing over her, his fist crushed around a roll of money, and his other hand leaning on a cane, tilting his body. He raised the fist filled with money, ready to hit her again.

"Stop it." The sound shocked even Bree. Katy's dad turned around, his face almost purple with beads of sweat from forehead to chin. Katy was on her bed, curled in a ball with a blanket clenched in her hands.

"Bree, no, get out of here," Katy said.

Her dad aimed his hand at Bree. "Is this the bitch who's been selling you this shit?"

"Leave her alone," Bree said. She shook from the blast of adrenaline and fear lighting her from within.

"You don't tell me what to do in my house."

"That's not your money."

He looked at the crumpled stack, then back to Bree. "Like hell, it isn't."

"It's not."

She knew she sounded like a petulant child. She knew he didn't care what she thought or what she told him to do.

"You get the fuck out of my house."

Bree turned on her heel and walked away. Katy's screech of agony hurt Bree in her bones. Katy must have felt her last chance walking away and leaving her. But that would never happen.

Bree went to the living room, where she hadn't been in a long time, but things were the same as they had been. A tall gun cabinet stood in the corner. Glass front to show a row of six rifles. A drawer below. She pulled open the drawer, the lock not engaged. Four handguns sat in custom-cut foam holders. beside each was a box of ammunition. She grabbed the first one she saw, a silver revolver. She lifted it, and it came out much heavier than she expected. She turned it in her hand and saw it had six rounds in the

190

cylinder. A loaded gun in an unlocked drawer. Sounded about right for him.

She moved quickly, churning her feet faster than her better judgment could catch up with her. When she returned to the door, his back was to her again. She held the gun in both hands, threaded both her index fingers next to the trigger.

"Drop the money and back away from her."

She nearly choked on the words, but she got them out, and he spun. His face fell when he saw the gun, and he teetered on his cane. It added insult that his own gun was pointed at him in anger.

"Drop. The. Money."

"You little piece of shit. You come into my house and threaten me? I could kill you and be totally justified. Self-defense. No cop would even arrest me. I could shoot you in the goddamn face."

Bree pulled her fingers back on the trigger, and a bullet blasted into the wall. His face began to lose its color.

"Let her get up, and don't move a fucking muscle."

Katy had her face burrowed into her blanket.

"Come on, Katy. Get up. We're leaving."

"You stay right there, Kate."

Bree thrust the gun out in front of her. It shook at the end of her arms.

"You think a cop would arrest *me*? Beating the shit out of your own daughter? Stealing her money? Threatening her with a gun. One that I took off of you to shoot you with."

"You lying little–"

"I'll say whatever the fuck I have to, and you won't say shit about it because you'll be dead, asshole."

Katy began to move, slithering off the bed and making sure to stay far enough away from her father that he couldn't grab her as she went past.

"Get the money," Bree told her. Katy stopped and turned back to her dad. If she reached for it, he could grab her. Bree saw her dilemma.

"Drop it," she said to him. "Now."

Father and daughter stood opposite each other, unmoving.

"Katy, come here. Get away from him." Katy scurried over to stand in the doorway with Bree.

"Now toss the money over here. Just do it."

"You can't get anywhere," he said. "You're kids."

"We're both adults. And as long as I have this gun, I can do whatever the hell I want. Now toss it here."

He closed his fist around the money and squeezed until she thought the bills would come leaking out between his fingers. Then he threw the roll like a baseball. It hit the wall next to the door and fell to the floor, unraveling and spilling bills at their feet. Bree kept the gun trained on him.

"Pick it up, Katy. All of it."

Katy did.

"Now you stay here unless you want a bullet."

Bree took a step backward. Katy broke and ran for the front door. Bree kept her eye on him as long as she could until she needed to turn the corner. He stayed still, his face angrily watching her go like he was making a mental list of all the ways he was going to torture her when he found them. His bad leg made it impossible for him to chase after them.

Katy left the door open as she went through it. Bree ran after her, keeping the gun. They got in the car, and she scrambled to turn the key like a final girl in a horror movie. As they pulled away, Bree saw Katy's dad limp into the doorway, watching them with a disturbing calm on his face.

Cleaning was never Carter's thing. The good news was the bodies didn't bleed nearly as much as he worried they would. Even the shorter one with the headshot. It helped that he moved as quickly as his injured leg would allow. He hobbled from the living room to the kitchen as Chester sniffed and inspected the two corpses on the floor.

Carter came back with a bucket, a roll of paper towels, and every can, bottle, and jar of anything chemical he found under the sink. First, he covered Dill's head in a garbage bag. Any more blood leaking out would collect inside. He did the same to Waco, wrapping six bags around him as best he could. He rolled the bodies over to the cellar door. A door he hadn't opened in more than five years. When he finally did, it smelled of mildew and stale air like a crypt, which felt about right.

There was no hope of his lifting the bodies down the steps on his bad leg, so he pushed and let the bodies tumble down into the darkness. Chester barked from behind him, thinking it a game, or perhaps warning him how stupid this was, leaving bodies in your basement. It was all Carter had right then.

He felt a compulsive need to get the place clean. To erase the whole thing from his house and from his mind.

He repositioned the rug, slid the couch a few inches left to cover where Waco had fallen, and left some blood that stained the wood. He righted the table and piled the pieces of the broken lamp in a heap with his foot, then went to get a dustpan to sweep it up and get rid of it. He made a mental note to get the lamp from the bedroom upstairs and swap it out. He took the gun and put it back in the case and put it and the box of shells in the closet. He set the guitar back in its case, like laying a baby down for a nap.

It took a solid half hour of frenzied work as he fought the slow drag of the pill the whole time, and by the end, Carter collapsed on the couch in a cloud of cleaning fluid fumes. Chester had paced behind him, showing worry, interest, and finally, boredom as he lay down and went to sleep while Carter made the last touches to his cleaning.

He expected to lay there and come up with a plan of what to do with the bodies, but his mind was so tired he fell immediately to sleep.

Carter woke with a jerk at Chester's barking. Then he heard a knock on the door. This one was a far cry from Bree's. This one was a man's hand, a heavy one, with authority.

"Mr. McCoy? Police."

He felt like he was going to melt through the couch, just sink into the earth like rainwater. Chester continued to bark.

"Police," the voice repeated. "I'd like to ask you a few questions."

Carter stood, swayed a little, but the sudden surge of adrenaline pushed aside the pill in his bloodstream. He went to the door and opened it a crack, keeping Chester back behind the door.

Brian DeFore smiled at him, but to Carter those teeth looked like knives. "Mr. McCoy?"

"Yes." He turned inside. "Chester, shut up." Chester went quiet.

"Detective DeFore. Mind if I ask you a few questions?"

"What about?"

"Oh, a few different things."

Carter could still smell the chemical tang in the air from his cleaning supplies. Ammonia, bleach, and fake lavender scent all mingled in the air.

"I s'pose so."

Carter figured he would ride it out as long as he could maintain the lie, but when he saw the end was coming, he'd spill. Keep Bree's name out of it. Take the rap, like they say on TV. He'd be dead by the time it went to trial anyway.

He pulled open the door, gestured to Chester. "He doesn't bite, just sounds like he might. He likes new people. 'Bout as old as me."

Chester started wagging his tail and, as he did when he got excited, blasted a puff of gas that neither man could ignore. Carter could've kissed the dog right then. His noxious fumes made a smoke screen for the cleaning chemicals. Plus, with this hanging in the air, the cop wouldn't want to stay for long.

DeFore bent down a little to pat Chester on the head as he moved by. "Good boy. Chester, you said?"

"Yeah. Sorry about the stink."

"Hey, we all do it, right?"

"He's perfected it, though."

Carter shut the door and exhaled, calming himself for what was to come. He felt strangely serene. If this was how it ended, then fine. This cop had done some good work to lead him here. Carter almost laughed out loud when he thought to himself, *I wonder which murder he's here about?*

"You didn't ask to see any I.D.," DeFore said.

"Do I need to?"

"No. I'm really a cop. It's just that most people these days aren't that trusting."

"I don't know if you noticed, but I'm from a different generation."

DeFore smiled. "I guess you are at that, Mr. McCoy." He settled on a spot on the floor where the boards creaked under his feet. "That your truck outside?"

"Yes, sir."

DeFore gave him another dagger smile and waved him off. "You don't have to bother with that sir stuff. We're just a couple of old-timers talking."

"Force of habit," Carter said. "And I'm a bit older than you."

DeFore took in the room as he walked, making observations, his eyes mostly on the walls, the shelves, the photos. Carter stood where Dill had fallen.

"So, that is your truck?" DeFore asked again.

"Yeah."

"Nobody else drives it?"

"No. Just me. She's kinda temperamental. I know how to get her going."

"I bet you do. You know anybody that lives at twelve sixteen Greenbriar?"

Carter gave it a bit of theatrical thinking. "Not that I know of."

"How about next door, twelve fourteen?"

"No."

DeFore paced a little more. Chester followed him, sniffing at his shoes.

"Reason I ask, I have your truck." He pointed. "That truck out there you said is yours, and nobody else drives it. I have it on traffic cameras going right by those addresses multiple times in the past few days."

"I like to get out and drive. Keeps me from being housebound. Gets lonely out here."

"All alone?" DeFore glanced at a photo of Ava.

"My wife passed several years ago."

"I see." He moved on to the next photo on the bookshelf. "No kids?"

"One. She passed a long while back."

"Audrey, right?"

Carter felt himself tense, worried it was a tell. But what father wouldn't tense when hearing the name of his dead daughter?

"That's right."

"Were you aware, Mr. McCoy, that the man accused of a role in your daughter's death, Justin Lyons, lived at twelve sixteen Greenbriar?"

"I knew it was out."

"Did you know where he lived?"

Carter folded his arms, took on a hard stance. "Far as I'm concerned, he should still be living up at the penitentiary."

DeFore started pacing again, letting Carter avoid the question. "Then did you know that Mr. Lyons was found dead in his home a few nights ago?"

Chester gave up following the new man and took his place on the couch.

"You want me to bust out crying for the man who killed my daughter?"

"I just asked if you knew about it."

"No." Carter used his anger to make it sound convincing, even to himself. "But now that I do know…good riddance."

DeFore nodded, satisfied with the answer, it seemed.

196

"You want a drink or something, detective? You woke me up, and I'm parched."

"No, thank you. I'm good. Sorry to wake you."

"You'll see someday. Naps kinda sneak up on you when you're my age."

DeFore watched him limp to the kitchen. He called after him, "Hurt yourself there?"

"Bad leg."

Carter poured himself a glass of water from the tap.

"Old war wound or something?" DeFore asked from the living room.

"No. Last week. Damn dog tripped me in the yard, and I fell on a stick. Near about went through my leg."

Carter returned to the living room and found DeFore standing right over where Dill had died. The rug covered the spot, but he suddenly doubted his cleaning skills.

"The thing is," DeFore said. "A man who lived in the house next door turned up dead not long after Justin Lyons. And both nights, your truck was seen in the vicinity."

Shit. He was here about both killings.

"Small town," Carter said. "Everything is the vicinity of everywhere else."

"That's true. But a coincidence like this…well, you understand that I had to follow up on it."

"It's your job." Carter took a drink.

"And with your connection to one of the victims—"

"I have no connection to Justin Lyons."

"Tangential it may be, but—"

"I got *no* connection to him."

DeFore lifted his hands in surrender. "Fair enough."

"They were neighbors. Had to know each other."

"You'd think, but there's no indication of that."

Carter shrugged. "Yeah, well, I'm not here to tell you how to do your job."

"Do you own a hunting rifle, Mr. McCoy?"

Carter knew the cop could see the hesitation. It was a blindside punch. He tried to keep his feet.

"I don't hunt."

"You have a hunting dog."

Carter waved the glass at the sleeping Chester. "Only thing he hunts these days is sleep and the occasional cheeseburger."

"I can see that."

DeFore had taken at least two full laps of the room, slowly and methodically.

"You mind if I take a look at your truck, Mr. McCoy?"

"Have at it. It's open. No need to lock it way out here. I believe I'm gonna get back to my nap."

"Thanks for your time."

"Not to worry. You gotta follow up on everything, I guess."

"That's true." DeFore went to the door, gave one last look around the room.

"Guess if you made it all the way out here to talk to an old man, it must mean you have no idea at all who killed those boys."

DeFore gave his sharpened smile again. "We have some ideas we're working on. Thanks again."

Carter stayed by the window and watched as DeFore gave a search of his truck. He worried he might have left a rifle shell on the floorboard, or some other stupid mistake, but DeFore walked away and got into his car after a few minutes.

Carter set the drink down, shoved Chester over to make room, and passed out on the couch.

When Katy finally stopped crying, she looked out the windshield.

"Where are we going?"

Bree kept her eyes on the road and her foot on the gas. "I know someone who can help us."

She had a gun, Katy's portion of the money, and a full tank of gas. Bree contemplated leaving town and heading west, but she knew he would come after them. She knew the money wasn't enough. She knew this place wasn't so easy to leave.

A dark bruise ringed Katy's left eye. Not her first. Yellowing bruises were hidden under her shirt.

"Jesus, Bree, I thought you were gonna kill him."

"Yeah? And what would you have done?"

Katy was silent for a while. Bree knew she was picturing her dad dead, shot through the heart by her best friend. A chain broken that kept them weighted down here, like prisoners.

"I don't know what I would've done."

"You'd have laughed and done a dance, that's what."

Katy watched a field of green go by out the window. "Maybe."

Bree turned up the long drive to Carter's farmhouse.

She knocked quickly and turned the knob, but the door was locked. So she knocked harder.

"Carter?"

He sat up when Chester's bark fell in sync with Bree's pounding.

"Fuckin' Grand Central Station in here."

At least he knew who it was this time, with all her hollering. He smoothed his hair a bit with his fingers as he shuffled to the door. Memories of his day came crashing back into his brain and nearly made him lose balance.

Carter unlocked the door and pulled it open. Bree was there, alone, looking panicked.

"That cop come see you too?" he asked.

"What? No. You gotta help me."

She pushed past him, and Chester stopped his barking when he saw who it was. He thumped his tail against the couch a few times, and she scratched at his head absently while she pleaded with Carter.

"My friend Katy is here, out in the car. She needs a place to stay. Her dad went fucking nuts and beat her up and tried to steal her money."

"Ho, slow down there. What's this got to do with me?"

"You need to help her. Help us."

He moved a few steps close to her. "Jesus H. Christ, Bree, haven't I helped enough?"

She sucked in a breath to plead her case, but stopped herself before she said anything more. She looked at the old man, and that's what he looked like now more than ever before. His hair askew, his leg unsteady beneath him, and his eyes tired and watery. Maybe he had done enough.

"This is the last thing, I promise."

He sighed and rolled his eyes as he made his way back to the couch. "I've had a hell of a day already, okay? I got some things I need to figure out." Like how and where to dispose of two dead bodies.

"Carter, one more thing, and I am out of your hair forever, I swear."

He let himself fall onto the seat. "You know a cop came to see me? A detective, asking questions about why my truck was seen near *your* house?"

"You don't want them to know why, do you?"

"Oh, for—this again? God dammit, Bree, I don't think you really understand how little I give a shit anymore. I'm already on a downhill slide to an open grave. All you're doing is putting a brick on the accelerator."

"Then help us because it's the right thing to do."

"How's that?"

"Because Katy's dad is an abusive asshole, and we both need to get the hell out of here so we can be safe."

"Bree." He sighed again, sounding tired. "You're the one keeping you here, you know that? You want out, get out. You don't need your mother's permission. You don't need Katy's permission. And you sure as hell don't need my help."

"I do, Carter." Tears came to her eyes. "I really do."

She did it again, reminding him of Audrey. His day had been so stressful, the medicine clouded his judgment. He was being harsh, and he knew it.

"I can give you some money," he said.

"I need a real favor."

"Money isn't real all of a sudden?"

"I need you to kill Katy's dad."

Carter pushed himself off the couch and walked toward the kitchen. "God dammit, Bree."

She followed him. "Last thing. Swear to God."

"I've had enough killing."

"But he deserves it."

Carter stopped, swiveled, and looked like he might topple over on his one bad leg. His long whiskers gave him a more serious look than when she first met him. The kindly grandpa was gone now. This face had seen and done things.

"I deserve it, Bree. I've murdered men. I deserve to die, and I'm gonna get my wish. But no more. No more blood on my hands."

"If you saw what he does to her."

Carter leaned against the counter, facing away from her, hands gripping the edge. He stared down into the sink. "No more."

Chester wandered into the kitchen, wondering if it was mealtime.

"Carter, you're the only one I have now."

He squeezed his eyes shut. Her words pierced him deeper than the pain in his gut that would soon kill him.

"If you help us, you'll never see me again. I get to go have a life. Katy too. Carter, nobody else in the world can help us."

He squeezed the counter harder.

"I'm gonna go get her."

He heard her sneakers squeak on the floor. He spun and nearly lost his balance. "No, Bree. No. Dammit."

She was gone, and he was left alone with his decision. Once you've gone so far, what more is a few more miles down the road. And once the sun goes down, darkness is darkness, right? Night doesn't get any more black the longer it goes on.

He looked at Chester. "I can't. I just can't."

Chester licked his chops, weary eyes studying Carter.

"I'm no killer."

Yes, you are, he thought. *And she knows it. That's why she's coming to you.*

He heard the front door open and close. Could hear Bree talk in a comforting tone to her friend as she eased her down into the armchair. Carter pushed off the counter and limped into the living room.

Bree was quiet now, her pleading tone gone. She moved timidly around Katy, not wanting to spook her.

"Carter, this is my best friend, K—"

"Katherine?"

Katy looked up through teary eyes at Carter, who stared back with a shock that loosened his face until it was slack and pale.

"Mr. McCoy?"

Bree pinched her face into a confused scowl. "You know each other?"

"What happened?" Carter asked.

Katy broke down in tears. She put her face into her hands.

"Wait, what the fuck?" Bree said. "How do you two know each other?"

"Her mother owns a restaurant," he said. "She waitresses there sometimes."

"Shit. Right, the Mesa Grande."

"I've been going there for years. I've seen Katherine grow up."

"Then you know her dad?"

"Eddie. Yeah."

He put a hand on Katy's shoulder, felt it lift and fall with her sobs.

"Does your mom know you're here?"

Katy shook her head as she lifted it from her hands. Her shiner glistened under the coating of tears.

"She's at work," Katy said.

Bree was pacing now, trying to piece together the new information. "What the...?"

"Your dad did that to you?" he asked, pointing to her eye.

Katy nodded. Slowly, she lifted her shirt to show fading bruises on her ribs. "After you attacked him, he came home and...he said he didn't like anyone telling him how to be a father or a husband. Said my mom wasn't allowed to kick him out of his own house."

He pushed her shirt down and covered her again. He lay his hand on her head, smoothed down her hair. Carter turned to Bree.

"This changes things."

FOUR

"Okay, here's how this is gonna go."

Carter had them at the kitchen table. He'd listened to Katy talk for a half hour, detailing the abuses and indignities from Eddie over the years. Not much of it was new to him, but coming from her mouth, it landed with an alcohol sting to his bloodstream.

He'd given them Cokes to drink. Bree had pushed for beer, but he refused her. Clear heads, that's what they needed. All of them. The pills were out. Let the pain sharpen his senses.

He'd asked how Ivana felt about it, though he thought he knew.

"She taught me Spanish," Katy said, "so we could talk around him, and he wouldn't understand."

Carter nodded. He'd seen them do it in the restaurant. Talking to each other like nobody else existed.

"She hates him, but she's scared. And the business is in his name. If she left him, she'd lose Mesa Grande."

"Well, the only way I do this is with her approval."

Katy shot her hand forward and put it on his arm, shoving her chair back until it scraped on the floor. Chester woke up with a start at the sudden noise.

"You can't. She'll say no. She can't know that I asked you to do this."

"I'll talk to her. I'll make her understand. But if she says no, I need to respect that."

Katy looked to Bree for help, but Bree had nothing to give. Katy slumped back into her seat.

"Okay."

"And the other thing," he said. "I do this, and you both leave town. For good. No looking back. You get far away from the trouble and the questions, and you start your new life."

Bree looked anxiously at Katy, wanting to hear her enthusiasm. Katy was slow to answer and squirmed in her seat.

"If Mom says it's okay."

"It's not like you'll never see her again. You just need to clear out and get on with your lives." Carter looked between the two girls. "You ever see a fox get loose from a trap?"

"No," Bree said.

"It doesn't look back. It might have had to chew off its own foot, but it doesn't look at the thing that trapped it. It just gets away. Runs. Far. That's what you need to do."

"Okay, Carter."

"Mr. McCoy?" Katy asked. "Thanks for helping us."

He tried but couldn't muster a smile. Just nodded his head and stood. Outside it was bottom-of-a-well dark, the crickets in full song.

"I'll go talk with your mother."

Nava stopped off at his desk to grab his water bottle before heading out. He saw that DeFore was back.

"Hey."

DeFore said hey back, but didn't look up from the papers he studied.

"Get anything from the red truck guy?"

DeFore finally tore his eyes from his paperwork and sat back in his chair. He looked tired.

"Not really. I don't know, though."

"What?"

"He didn't shed a tear about Justin, which is understandable. I couldn't tell if he already knew, though. And he was cagey about some of my questions."

"Acting squirrely, huh? Think he's behind this?"

"It's not a neat fit. Old guy like that. Knew one vic, sort of, but not the other. If there's a connecting thread, I don't see it yet. But," he threaded his fingers behind his head and leaned back. "I don't see anything else here, either. He's the closest I got to a suspect."

"What's next? Search warrant? Maybe find the gun?"

"I'm thinking about it. Can't hurt, right? Hate to harass a senior citizen, but a search won't be too bad on him."

"If he's giving you a vibe, I say go for it. Trust your gut."

"y gut says I'm hungry."

Nava gave a quick salute. "See you tomorrow."

"I'll go to the courthouse tomorrow and dig up a judge to

"

Nava took a step to the door, then turned back. "You want to come over for dinner? Maria wouldn't mind."

DeFore studied the look on his partner's face. "Is that sympathy because you think I'm just gonna go home alone and heat up another frozen dinner, or do you really want to spend *more* time together?"

"Just being friendly. You spend too much time here."

"Got nowhere else to be." DeFore knew how pathetic that sounded the second it came out of his mouth. "But I'm fine. I'll get a hot meal, not just some microwave thing. I promise you. Once this case is over, I'll come by."

"I don't mean to make your bachelor life sound like it needs my help, y'know?"

"Yeah, most married guys would be jealous."

"Not this one. I couldn't handle dating these days."

DeFore shook his head, thinking of how daunting the prospect of setting up a profile on some dating website would be. "Yeah. I think I'll stick to case jackets for now."

On his way out the door, Nava called back, "Gonna make headlines if this old guy is our shooter."

"Gonna make national news."

DeFore heard Nava from the hallway give a polite greeting to Chief Winters. A moment later, he appeared at the door.

"Got a second, Brian?"

"We're close, Chief. I feel it."

"That's good. Anything I can share with people. They're asking."

"Not yet. But trust me. I think I'm headed down the right path here."

Chief Winters leaned against the door. His suit jacket and tie were both wrinkled, and DeFore wished he also wore a more formal outfit so he could feel as professional and confident as he tried to sound.

"I can always call in some help. More resources."

DeFore knew what that meant. Someone from a city who dealt with ten homicides a month and who would also take over his investigation and bring it across the goal line and take all the credit.

"No, thanks. Soon, Chief. I promise. Soon."

"Promises aren't always easy to keep, DeFore."

Chief Winters knocked twice on the door, his exit sound. He left DeFore wondering if he was really on the right path or not.

The windows of the restaurant framed her like a TV screen. Ivana wiped a cloth over the counter, her face sagging and tired at the end of the day and with nobody else to put on an appearance for, she let herself be as tired as she felt.

Carter stood outside, watching her for a while. Eddie was home, making her clean up after a long day of cooking, waitressing, and ringing every order into the cash register, knowing that the money wasn't really hers. Seemed more like indentured servitude from where Carter stood.

Eddie was an asshole, but would she go for the plan? He'd crossed another line he never knew was there. After killing once, he leaped over the line into killing twice. Then killing in self-defense. Now, he had to convince a woman he admired and respected for her permission to kill her husband. With the blessing of her daughter.

But Ivana knew how difficult leaving him would be. If she really did go talk to a lawyer, they'd tell her the same and in more detail. How Eddie controlled her life and her money, her business, and ultimately, her daughter. He'd built a web around her, and she was caught in its sticky threads.

He thought of the first time Audrey ever said, "I hate you." Nearly every teenager does it. They all think it. Probably all think *this old bastard would be better off dead*. Better for the kid, anyhow. But how many really meant it? How many had the cause to wish their own father dead and have someone else agree?

Clearly, Eddie wasn't going to learn.

Carter knocked on the glass. Katy and Bree waited in the truck in the far corner of the parking lot. He didn't want Ivana to see her there yet.

It took a moment for her to recognize him and when she did a smile came to her face, despite the exhaustion. She wiped her hands on her apron and unlocked the door. The diner was quieter than he'd ever heard it. None of the usual Tejano music filling the gaps between muffled talk, bursts of laughter, the metallic tap of flatware like a swarm of insects in the air. Carter figured Ivana probably liked this time of night in her place. Customers gone, Eddie at home and out of her mind. Maybe it made the extra work not so bad.

"Carter, what are you doing here so late? Did you skip dinner?"

He did not meet her smile, and she sensed something was wrong.

"Can we talk, Ivana?"

"What is it?"

"Inside?"

"Are you okay, Carter?"

"Let's sit down. I'll make coffee for you for a change."

He needed so many instructions about where things were—the filters, the grounds, the cups— she might as well have done it herself, but he made her sit at the counter and just point to where to find the supplies. Finally, when the coffee was made, he set two cups in front of them and sat next to her, shoulder to shoulder, so he wouldn't have to look at her face.

"Katherine came to my house tonight," he said. "With her friend, Bree."

"She did? Is she okay?"

"She will be." He sipped. "Had a run-in with Eddie again."

Ivana looked like she'd been hit with one of Carter's abdominal pains.

"I hope I didn't make things worse with what I did to him," Carter said.

Ivana hadn't touched her coffee. "How could it get worse?"

"That's what I want to talk to you about."

"Carter, I know you want to help but—"

"I can help." He finally turned to her and met eyes with hers. "I can put an end to it."

Katy and Bree huddled together despite the extra space on the bench seat of the truck.

"Is he really gonna do it?" Katy asked.

"He did it for me," Bree said.

"He really killed Chris?"

Bree nodded.

"My mom's gonna freak out."

"No, she won't. She hates his guts."

"So why hasn't she done it herself?"

Bree squeezed her tighter. "Why didn't I do Chris myself? It's not that easy."

They couldn't see anything but the lights of Mesa Grande. The rectangular sign on the roof with the clipart cacti and an orange sunset. The neon sign in the window that read *Authentic Mexican*, even though Ivana wasn't from Mexico. It's what people wanted to hear. And inside, either Carter was finally telling her what she wanted to hear, or frightening her into the arms of the police.

"Carter can do it because of his situation," Bree said.

"His what?"

"He's dying."

Katy turned her neck to face Bree in the tight confines of their embrace.

"He told me," Bree said. "Some disease. That's why he killed my neighbor. He can do it because he's almost out of time, and he can do something good before he goes."

"How is killing people something good?"

"Look at it. It is. Look at who it is. Look at who it's helping. It is."

They kept watch on the diner, looking for a sign.

Carter waited for her to scream, to run out, to reach for the phone and call the police or warn her husband. She sat there, motionless, her coffee still untouched.

"And Katherine wants this?"

"She's young. She thinks she wants it. But I won't do it if it's not what you want."

"Sometimes you can say you want something, even think it, wish for it…then when you have it handed to you…you can't be sure."

"I know exactly what you mean."

Carter felt she might start to cry. "It's not so easy," she said. "To leave him."

"I know."

"He owns this place. The bank accounts are in his name. I can't just steal away in the night like some women can."

"You've done enough leaving. It's his turn now."

Ivana stood and walked slowly behind the counter, bent down to a small cooler, and came back with a beer in her hand. She put the neck into a bottle opener attached to the underside of the counter and levered the cap off with a crack and fizz. She tipped the bottle and drank for a long time.

"Katherine," Ivana started. "She's been taking drugs. I think to dull the pain."

Carter stayed quiet and watched her work it all out behind her eyes.

"You had a daughter," she said.

Carter nodded.

"And you lost her."

He nodded again.

"And you'd do anything to get her back? Anything to keep her from the harm that came to her?"

Slowly, he nodded his head. She understood now.

"And you would do this for me?"

"Would you believe it won't be my first time?"

She raised both eyebrows and then took another swig of her beer.

"You think it will work? Your plan?"

"I think it will. No guarantees. But even if it doesn't, it's only me who goes down. You and Katherine are in the clear no matter what."

"But I don't want you to go to jail."

"It's not that big a deal, trust me."

"It is a big deal."

He opened his mouth to tell her about his short time, then shut it again. He took a sip of coffee instead, then said, "Just trust me."

Ivana stood for a long time. Her hair had come loose from its braid in fraying edges. She chewed her lip. Her unpainted nails tapped the side of the beer bottle.

She moved close to the counter where he'd seen her a thousand times, but her face had changed. She was not there to serve anyone. She looked Carter in the eye, tipped her bottle forward, and tapped it against the edge of his cup. The clink echoed in the empty diner, different from the normal clinking of glasses and scraping of forks on plates. They both knew what it meant. Neither smiled. They were serious, somber. But they both drank.

Carter left Katy and Bree with Ivana. Katy had collapsed into tears and fallen into her mother's arms when she saw her. They clung to each other as Carter knew they had done the same many nights before, cowering in fear from the man who was supposed to love them. Bree stood by and watched, a visible jealousy and longing for a mother-daughter relationship she never had.

Carter explained that when it was done, the girls would be leaving. Going west. Ivana might not see her daughter for a long time, and she had to be okay with that. Ivana nodded and held Katy tighter. She spoke to her in Spanish.

"You will be okay?"

Katy nodded.

"You will be strong?"

She continued nodding.

He pictured himself as no different from a doctor asking a family if it was time to pull the plug. These two women knew what was best for Eddie, for their family. He asked again before he left.

"I walk out that door, there's no going back." He met both women's eyes. "Speak now or forever hold your peace."

"Isn't that what they say at weddings?" Bree said.

"It's what you say when you want there to be no misunderstanding that this is serious business."

Ivana nodded first, then Katy. Eddie's fate was sealed.

Truth was, he probably could have used their help. With his bad leg, getting the two bodies up out of the basement was a chore that nearly did him in. After the first body, Waco, was up, Carter had to take twenty minutes and nurse his aching gut. He now knew the feeling of being knifed with a serrated blade right through his liver. For the first time, he wanted to know the nine-syllable name just so he could curse it out loud.

"Can't blame some disease, though," he said to Chester. "When it's really my own damn body that's killing me." Chester hadn't laid down, which was rare for him. He could tell Carter was in distress. Plus, the dead body on the floor was fascinating to smell.

Carter finished a bottle of Coke, let out a large, cathartic belch, then went down for Dill.

"Your own damn fault," he said to the corpse. He pulled and moved the weight up one more step. "Trying to shake down an old man. What the hell did I expect, though, from a dumbass who sells drugs to kids?"

Chester waited at the top of the stairs, tail wagging, wondering what Carter was bringing him to play with next.

He lifted and felt a stab of pain through his abdomen. It met in the middle, right behind his spine, with a pain in his back muscles. He had to set Dill down and sit on a step. The body slid down six steps, wiping out ten minutes of progress. Carter was sweating, and he wondered if he'd have enough strength for the second part of his plan.

He stood again after the pain had passed and moved quickly to the top step. He let Dill roll onto Waco, and they lay there like two enchiladas on a plate.

Chester was no help at all.

Carter pulled the truck up to the front porch and backed the tailgate as close as he could. He dragged the two bodies out and was able to slide them into the bed of the truck from the porch. Chester was so curious and worked up that Carter decided to bring him along in the truck.

He went back inside, splashed cold water on his face, then got the rifle and the case and tossed it in back with the two bodies.

"C'mon then," he said to Chester. The dog jogged to the truck and stood waiting to be lifted inside. When he got on the bench seat, he curled up and laid down, snoring almost immediately.

Carter stuffed Dill's pistol between the seat and the back cushion. He bumped down the drive and headed west.

Parked outside Ivana's house, he felt a strange comfort in the fact that it hadn't gotten any easier to contemplate killing a man. Carter had been there a good fifteen minutes listening to Chester snore on the seat beside him. He worried slightly that someone would come by and see the bodies in the bed of his truck, but not enough to make him get out yet. He'd covered the two with an old sheet, but Carter had learned in recent years that someone his age was nearly invisible to most other people. Especially one alone. Eating alone, shopping alone, browsing the library alone—people gave him a wide berth like they were afraid his age would rub off on them and take years off their lives.

He had a plan. He'd given Ivana a story to tell the police and felt confident she would deliver it truthfully. She had the most to gain from this, even if it meant losing her daughter for a time.

The front door opened, and Eddie stepped out, holding a plastic garbage bag sagging with weight. The limp in his leg was pronounced and Carter nearly smiled at thinking how he and Eddie had that in common. He walked the trash bag to the curb and put it inside a can, then turned back to his door, his leg hitching along behind him. Ordinary chores done by all men, good or bad. We all do mostly the same things, thought Carter. It's that little one percent difference between us that makes someone an asshole and someone a saint.

It also depends a lot on where you sit. The police would consider Carter one of the bad guys now. Chris's mother. Anyone who might have loved Justin, though he doubted there was anyone left on this earth who did.

If you're holding a gun on someone, you each have your own take on who is the bad one.

He pulled Dill's handgun from between the cushions of the seat, pat Chester on the head, and said, "Hold down the fort." Chester lifted his head and grumbled.

Carter walked to the door, noticing an unkempt lawn. His own at home had overgrown, but he had no plans to ever mow grass again. But Eddie didn't know his time was short, so he had no excuse.

He thought what he might say. The same problem had vexed him with Justin. Do it quick. If he had learned anything, or if he had any sort of pattern to this behavior, it was that. Don't linger. This isn't a conversation. Not a time for lessons to be learned. Just pull down the curtain and shut off the lights on this man.

Carter looked up and down the street. He needed time after the deed to complete the plan, so he couldn't draw a lot of attention. He needed to get the bodies inside and stage the scene. Couldn't exactly do that with neighbors watching.

There were two metal chairs on the porch, the kind that rocked a little on their pipe legs. Two cushions dark with mold on the edges covered the seats. He lifted one and bent it around the gun like an upside-down taco. It would muffle some of the shot, at least. Enough? He had no way of knowing.

He grabbed the second cushion and tried to sandwich it on top to make two layers of padding. It was awkward, and he feared it might mess with his aim, but he went with it, pinching the cushions below the gun. A narrow gap allowed the barrel to be unobstructed, otherwise his hand was covered by four inches of foam padding and yellow and orange striped fabric.

He could see every black eye Ivana tried to hide behind makeup over the years. He and Ava used to talk about it. "I think her husband mistreats her," she would say. "It's none of our business," he would say. What would she think now? She'd barely recognized the man she was married to for more than forty years.

"She ain't here, and I am, so let's do this."

He realized he couldn't knock on the door and hold the cushions in place, so he kicked at it with the toe of his boot. Three hard kicks, and then he took a single step back.

Eddie was angry when he came to the door. Seemed like a good way for him to go out of this world.

Carter fired twice, quickly. Both shots caught Eddie in the chest. The sounds were quieter than he expected. The cheap cushions did their job well.

Eddie fell back into the house in nearly the same way as Justin, though Eddie was bigger and fell harder. Carter gave a glance left and right to see if any lights came on in any windows, but the street stayed quiet except for Chester's excited bark from inside the truck.

"Shush," he said.

Eddie wasn't dead immediately. Carter dropped the cushions and stepped inside, closing the door behind him. Eddie was trying to crawl backward, his hands under his hips. He was gasping for air, and Carter knew his lungs had been hit. Must have missed his heart, though. He looked up at Carter with a real fear he hadn't seen before. In their other confrontations, Eddie retained a bit of defiance, but now he seemed to know this was it.

He was panting like a dog now, using up whatever precious oxygen he had in him. Carter started looking around to see where he might place Dill and Waco. Eddie backed into the bookcase against the back wall. The books there were dusty, and there were more knick-knacks than books. A bronze horse, a framed photo of the 2010 Super Bowl when Eddie got tickets to see his beloved Packers and left Ivana to work alone that weekend.

With nowhere else to go, Eddie stopped. He looked like he had questions for Carter, but didn't have the air to ask them. Carter felt like he had a lot to say to Eddie, but nothing came to mind. Both men knew why he was there. Both knew why this was happening. Both were equally as surprised that it was Carter behind the gun.

Carter tapped his foot impatiently, waiting for Eddie to go still. The color began fading from Eddie's face, and Carter noticed a small pool of blood forming underneath him. His time was coming. Carter felt comfortable enough to walk away from him for a moment.

He went into the garage and turned on the overhead light. It was a crowded space; one wall had restaurant supplies. One wall held a tool chest, table saw, a shop vac. Carter's eyes landed on what he wanted on the restaurant side. A dolly for moving the heavy boxes of supplies. He wheeled it back into the house.

Eddie hadn't moved. His chest still rose and fell, but the rise was short. His eyes were unfocused now. The questions had all been answered.

Carter dropped the gun and wheeled the dolly outside.

It made moving the bodies so much easier. He knew his back would be killing him tomorrow from his exertion to get them into the truck. He might have to relent and take another of his pills tonight, but his leg moved well, the wound on its way to being healed and to put this all behind him.

He laid out the two drug dealers closer to the door, facing Eddie. He wiped the handgun and then pressed Dill's fingers onto it before letting it fall to the floor beside his open hand. He went to the truck and got his dad's rifle. He removed it from the case and put the case in the hall closet behind some heavy winter coats. He set the rifle beside Eddie and pulled two spent shells from his pocket. He'd fired them out behind his house before he left, following every detail of his plan.

He let them drop to the floor, then stepped back. He looked at the scene. It made sense. Two men come to the door, a shootout ensues, all parties are hit. The gun by Eddie links him to the other two killings, and case closed.

Ivana had her story set. Eddie found out about Chris selling drugs to Katy. She would have to admit to that, even let her room be searched and find traces of the drugs, but in the scheme of things, her transgression was so minor they would likely ignore that. He hoped.

So Eddie went to kill Chris to help protect his daughter, whom he loved, she would say. But he went to the wrong house and killed Justin Lyons instead. Nobody they would bring to a trial could testify that Eddie was a smart man.

Realizing his mistake, he went back and followed Chris, killing him and dumping his body. When Dill, Chris's boss, found out, he came here to exact revenge and ended up being shot by Eddie, but not before Dill could get a fatal shot in himself.

It fit like a puzzle to Carter. There might be a missing piece, but he couldn't see it. And if it came back to him somehow, so be it. The detective, DeFore, would have some figuring to do, but he seemed smart enough.

Carter left the door open a bit when he left. He didn't see any lights on. Nobody standing on their porch and checking on an unusual noise. This might work.

He got in the truck. Chester grumbled again and lifted his head for a moment before settling back down. Carter wondered about more traffic cameras, but he couldn't help it. This would either work or it wouldn't. Time would tell. Time would tell a lot of things soon.

Bree announced that Katy was sleeping over. She didn't stop to see Mama's response. It hadn't been unusual for a sleepover in the past, but in recent years, Eddie had cracked down on Katy leaving the house. Still, Katy's presence was a familiar one to Mama.

She turned in her chair, watching them as they moved quickly down the hall.

"Did you bring something home for dinner?" Mama asked. Bree ignored the question, and Mama heard the door slam. She huffed out a breath and reached for the phone to order delivery.

Bree and Katy both climbed onto Bree's bed. They sat facing each other, cross-legged and holding hands. They hadn't said much on the drive over, and they said nothing now. Ivana had hugged them both and sent them home while she waited at the restaurant, giving Carter time to finish his task.

Now Bree and Katy held each other until their knuckles turned white, like grasping for a solid structure to hold on to. Shelter in a storm.

Bree saw the fear in Katy's eyes. She knew it. She felt the same way after she sent Carter out after Chris, but she knew it had to be worse for Katy.

"We're gonna be out of here," she said. "We have enough money. We can make it there. We won't have as much time to wait around and get a job, but we can find something temporary quick until we get real jobs. Work at a Starbucks or something."

"I have waitressing experience."

"See? Everyone always needs waitresses. I bet they tip good in California,

226

too. Not like around here."

"And I speak Spanish. That will help."

"Right." She smiled at Katy. "It's gonna work out. We're gonna get out of here."

Katy didn't look reassured. "My mom, though."

"She'll be fine. Do you know anyone tougher?"

Katy shook her head.

"Why did he have to be such an asshole?"

"Why do any of them?"

Bree opened her phone and found a playlist. Sad sounding music played. Seemed appropriate. They each let it fill the background.

"This is…," Katy said. "I mean…shit."

"Yeah. I know."

"When do you think we'll hear?"

"I don't know."

"You think he'll really do it?"

"Yeah. He will."

Katy pushed hair out of her face. "What's with that guy?"

"I don't know. But I'm glad I met him."

Carter opened the back door and let Chester run out into the night. He walked with him into the tall grass. He felt it tickle his calves as he walked, and Chester sniffed in the darkness. A half-moon overhead lit the yard in a dim, milky glow.

"I don't like it, boy," he said, though Chester was too far away to hear him. "The way it comes so natural. It's like picking up the guitar and your fingers finding the chords to a song you've never played. You just know it, somehow, inside you, and it comes out. I wish it weren't that easy for me to do."

He looked up into the night sky, at the pinpricks of light, and thought of himself up there in a few weeks or months. A soul floating in the black parts between the stars. He hoped it all ended when he did. He didn't want to be a lost consciousness, remembering and thinking and regretting all the things he'd done for eternity. He wanted the black to be as complete and wide as the space between those stars.

"I mean, shit, did what I did for seventy-two years before now stand for something? Or is this all I am at the end? It can't wipe out everything else, right?"

Chester was across the yard, nose down and moving the grasses in a slow swaying dance around his head. The dog had a whole life before this. One Carter would never know about. It didn't mean this was all this Chester amounted to. Old and tired and gassy. We aren't only what we've become. We're the culmination of a life lived. Good and bad. Mistakes and accomplishments.

When Bree and Katy are settled out west, when Ivana can leave work and

228

go home without worrying what awaits her, those are the weights that will balance what he's done. He knew the scales needed a little more on their side.

A misting rain began to fall. He went inside, leaving the door open for Chester to come inside whenever he was done.

There was no faking when Ivana went next door and asked Mrs. Conway to call the police. She woke the elderly lady and had trouble getting her to understand through the sobs and her accent that her husband was shot dead in her house. She stayed on the porch, getting soaked in the wet night air as the clouds continued to give up only a thick mist of droplets, holding back the real raindrops.

Even expecting it when she drove up, it was shocking to see. Eddie, with his open eyes and slack jaw, the pool of blood under him. Two more bodies in the entryway of her home.

Officers arrived quickly. They asked her a long list of questions, and she gave them brief answers through sobs and choking tears. They didn't need to know they were tears of happiness that it was all finally over.

She was taken down to the station, where she met with homicide detective DeFore. He looked as if he'd been rousted out of bed. He brought her coffee and sat with her.

"Do you need anything else?"

"No," she said and set the coffee aside.

"Do you have any idea who might have done this?"

She told him about Katy and the drugs. About how Eddie had said he was going to kill the dealer, but she didn't think he was serious about it.

"And where is your daughter now? I didn't see her name on the report."

"Sleeping over at a friend's. Her best friend."

As the details came out, DeFore saw the pieces fall into place. A half-hour after he started interviewing Ivana, Nava came in looking equally unrested.

"Excuse me, will you?" He said to Ivana.

She nodded and asked, "How much longer?"

"Not long."

"I need to call my daughter."

"You go ahead while I talk to my partner." He pointed to the phone on his desk.

Nava and DeFore stepped into an interrogation room.

"Waiting on ballistics from that rifle at the scene," Nava said. "But do we really need them?"

DeFore shook his head. "It all fits. Tight as a drum."

"Dad out for revenge?"

"They find anything in the house?"

"Girl's bedroom had a pipe and some residue. Looks like she's been using, so that tracks."

"He took care of Dill for us."

"Paid a price for it, though."

"Got off two lucky shots for a guy getting shot at himself."

Nava nodded and chewed his lip. "You not buying something here?"

DeFore continued to puzzle it out in his head. "I don't see anything missing. But when was the last time you had it handed to you on a platter?"

"Never. But hey, first time for everything, right?"

Katy burst into tears when she heard the news. Ivana told her she was getting a hotel for the night, but for Katy to stay with Bree. In the morning, they could talk about when she should leave.

"*Te amo*," Ivana said.

"*Te amo, mama.*"

"It's over. Everything's going to be okay."

"You promise?"

Ivana paused. She hated lying to her daughter. "I hope so."

The rain started falling in earnest, and Carter didn't leave the house all the next day. He stayed off his leg, left the back door open for Chester, and read until he finished the book he'd started. On the back page, it announced the next one in the series, but Carter figured he'd leave it there. Stories will go on without him, he figured. Might as well get used to it and not leave one half-read.

Bree quit her job and asked for her last payment in cash. The manager said he couldn't do that, and she called him a tool. She knew if the check came to her house after she'd left, Mama would cash it, and she'd never see that money.

"Whatever," she told Katy. "Let her have it. A parting gift."

"Did you tell her you're leaving?"

"Fuck no. She's gonna wake up in that chair, and she'll be all alone, and she'll have to fucking do something for herself for a change."

"Well, you've got me," Katy said.

They hugged, and Bree thought to herself how she hated not having a dad and not having a mother that she liked, but no matter what, no matter how jealous she was of Katy's relationship with her mom, she was glad she never wanted to kill her father. It was small, but it was the small things that kept her looking forward.

Wednesday morning, Carter visited the cemetery, Chester in tow. The rain had stopped, and the sky overhead was a flat slab of concrete-gray. He stood over his two girls and shoved his hands in his pockets.

"I honestly don't know if you'd be proud or not," he said. "I go back and forth myself. I talked to Ivana on the phone, and she said it went well with the police, and she thanked me. *Thanked* me, for God's sake. That didn't sit right, but if it made her feel better..."

He reached down and lifted a dead leaf off the grass. He tossed it away, but the breeze blew it back where it was, so he picked it up again and put it in his pocket.

"I stopped taking those damn pills. They made me loopy. I figure I got what's coming my way, pain-wise. Might as well face it head-on. I gotta own up to the things I've done. I didn't get lost in a bottle when you left us." He turned to face Audrey. "I was always proud of that. I know it's not asking much, but a lot of guys don't fare so well. And this is the same thing. I can't knock myself out and not face it. Any of it. And there's a lot of weight coming down on me. But we made it before." He turned back to Ava's name, carved in stone. "It was a hell of a lot easier with you next to me, babe."

He let himself sit on the verge of tears for a long while. He knew if he tried to speak again, he would lose it. Chester wandered over and put his head against Carter's leg, and he scratched the old dog behind the ears, thankful that he had someone with him.

Carter drove to the Grand Oak retirement home. Talking to headstones only got you so far. He needed a real human. He got out of the truck and lifted Chester out of the cab. He considered it for a second, then clicked his tongue and said, "Come on now."

There was a girl at reception in a white uniform. He didn't recognize her. "May I help you?" she said.

"Just here to see a friend. I usually know where to find him."

She looked down at Chester. "Sir, you can't have pets in here."

"He's a therapy dog."

The receptionist looked as if she might say something to prolong the argument, but she let her breath out and mumbled, "Whatever," as she waved them by.

Chester didn't know where to point his nose at all the new smells. Same smells Carter thought of as a prelude to death, Chester smelled in them a whiff of new adventures. Ken was on a little two-seater couch against a side wall. Two women were at the puzzle table, but they weren't placing any pieces, just staring through each other.

Carter let Chester walk up and lay his cold nose on Ken's hand.

"Who's this then?" Ken said.

"His name is Chester." Ken ran his hand over Chester's head. Chester sniffed Ken's sleeve, his pant leg, his armpit, the chair. Carter thought about asking if Ken knew who he was, but decided he didn't really want to know the answer.

"I guess you've been replaced as my best friend," Carter said and smiled

235

as he did so Ken would know he was joking. Ken continued to pet Chester and keep the dog entertained with a bouquet of smells.

Carter sat next to Ken on the couch.

"I've done some things, Ken." He let out a small snorting laugh. "I guess you could say that."

"Good things?"

"Depends on which side of the equation you're on, I guess." Carter watched Ken focus on the dog like he hadn't seen him focus on anything in quite a while. "Yeah," he said. "Good things."

"World still spins, doesn't it?"

"Yeah. World still spins."

"Makes you wonder if any of the shit we worried about mattered even a little bit."

Carter nodded. "We are a species prone to worry."

Ken turned from Chester and looked at Carter. He laid a hand on his wrist and gripped firmly. "You done good."

"You don't even know what I've done."

Ken smiled yellow teeth at him. "Is she happy?"

Carter had a feeling Ken meant Ava. Again, he didn't want to know for sure.

"Yeah. She's happy." Carter thought it was true. They'd all be happy. If not today, then someday. At least they'd get to see someday.

"Then you done good, Carter." Ken gave his wrist a final squeeze and then went back to petting Chester. Carter almost opened his mouth to something, but stopped.

"Excuse me."

Carter looked up, and the two women from the puzzle table stood nearby. They were stooped, wrinkled, gray in pallor but with gold bracelets that hung off their wrists big as hula hoops.

"May we pet your dog?"

"Of course. His name is Chester."

Blank stares were replaced by smiles revealing false teeth. The bracelets rattled as they each took an ear and rubbed, cooing and sighing and calling him a good boy. Chester leaned his head back and smiled. If heaven had a smell, to Chester, this was it. Carter noticed a man in a wheelchair rolling close and then one of the interns coming in from the next room, angling for Chester with a smile that pushed out his cheeks.

Goddamn miracles, dogs.

He met Ivana at the restaurant at three in the afternoon, after the lunch rush. Bree and Katy were there, too, by his request. He wasn't sure what their reaction would be to him, but he was greeted with cautious smiles.

"You don't think I'm some kind of monster?" he asked.

"No," Ivana said. "You are a kind man. A brave man."

He waved it away. "Okay, enough with that." He turned to Bree. "How you doing, kid?"

"We leave first light tomorrow morning."

He nodded. "About that." Carter reached into his back pocket and removed an envelope. He handed it over to Bree. "This is for you both."

Bree opened the seal and saw a thick stack of cash. She looked to Carter with questions in her eyes.

"I sold that old guitar of mine. Turned out it was worth some money."

She thumbed through the bills. "Carter, there's…a lot of money here."

"Eight thousand dollars." Katy let out an involuntary laugh. "I tried to get him to go ten, but he wanted to give me seven, so we met there at eight. Plus, I made him give me one of his cheap guitars so I still had something to play."

"You didn't have to do that."

"You need a decent start, you two. Can't do that on hopes and dreams alone. I don't want you staying at shithole motels on your way out to the coast."

Bree hugged him. He nearly broke out in tears, thinking how she was the same size, and wrapped her arms around the same parts of him as Audrey had. He thought he'd forgotten that feeling, but it came back to him like an electric shock.

He looked at Ivana when Bree broke the hug. "And you, young lady."

"Oh, Carter, no. No money."

"My pockets are empty," he said. "But listen. I had a few things changed around. As you know, I'm not long for this place."

Tears began to well in Ivana's eyes.

"I put you down in my will to get the house when I go. It ain't worth much, but it's something. You do with it what you want. Sell it, live in it, let it go to rot. Up to you."

"Oh, Carter."

"One condition, though. The dog comes with it. You gotta look after him as long as he's around."

She smiled through the tears. "Of course. Of course, I will."

"And also, you gotta make me some enchiladas right now."

Everyone could move again. Light, nervous laughter, and smiles filled the place. The same old songs played low, and the smells were so familiar it nearly made Ava appear. Carter had known for a while now, but in that moment it really sank in as he looked toward his usual booth and saw a glow of light where Ava used to sit, that not all ghosts are frightening. And being haunted is another word for being reminded of a memory.

"And a horchata, *por favor*."

"I got it," Katy said and went to pour his drink.

The new guitar wasn't the same. It was fine, but something was missing.

"This one's probably better for me," Carter said to Chester. "I'm not so good. That other one was wasted on me."

He plucked out his chords anyway as a slow and steady rain fell outside. The sun hadn't come out between rain storms, and the ground was saturated and soft. He kept a towel by the back door for when Chester would come inside with muddy paws and wet fur that made the whole house smell. Carter left the windows open and let the warm, wet air inside to drive out the smell of wet dog with the fresh smell of summer grass.

He checked the clock. Bree and Katy would be gone by now, rumbling that old car of hers out of the county toward the state line headed West. He hoped the old bucket of bolts could make it all the way to California, or if they needed any repairs, his money would get them through.

There was a knock on the door. Bree was gone. Ivana would be at the restaurant. He stayed behind the closed door and asked, "Who is it?"

"Detective DeFore. Can I see you, Mr. McCoy?"

Carter opened the door and saw DeFore there alone, an umbrella perched over his head. "May I come in? Nasty out here."

Carter widened the door and let him pass by. DeFore left the umbrella on the porch. Chester looked up, but didn't bark.

"What brings you all the way out here in the rain?" Carter asked as if he didn't know.

"Mind if we sit?"

Carter thought about asking him for a warrant, but there were no squad cars, no uniformed officers waiting with cuffs. He waved a hand toward the kitchen and followed DeFore in.

"I don't have coffee or nothing. Wanna Coke?"

"No, thanks. I'm fine."

They both sat facing each other, and DeFore took his time wiping water away from the nape of his neck and his forehead with a handkerchief.

Carter nodded toward him. "My dad used to carry one of those everywhere. Gone out of fashion, though."

"Guess I'm not a very fashionable guy," DeFore said.

"Police always were squares."

"That's me."

He folded his wet handkerchief and put it away in his pocket. "So," he said. "I wanted to update you on what we talked about before."

"On the murders?"

"Yes."

Carter offered nothing, waited to see what DeFore had to say.

"Seems like we wrapped it up. There was another shooting, and we found the murder weapon for the others. An angry father out for revenge on the men who sold drugs to his daughter."

"Scumbags."

"Right. I agree. Would have been nice to put them on trial and convict them, though."

"Didn't they get what they deserved?"

DeFore looked at Carter like he was trying to read his thoughts. "I guess they did."

"So why tell me? I could have read it in the paper."

"Like I said, I wanted to keep you informed since we'd had our other discussion."

"Well," Carter folded his arms across his chest. "Good for you, it's all wrapped up. Maybe you'll get a promotion out of it."

DeFore smiled and leaned back in his chair. Just a couple of old pals talking. "There's a few weird things."

Carter tried to keep his muscles from stiffening. "Yeah?"

"Like the two bodies at the scene—the M.E. says they died much earlier than the third vic. The shooter. And they didn't leave any blood at the scene."

Carter worked to keep his voice flat. "Is that really an exact science?"

"It is, yes. Very much so."

DeFore let a silence settle over them.

Carter shifted in his seat, the chair creaking a bit. "That the only thing?"

"Yeah, just about. Little things, but it ties up pretty well in the end. Nice bow on top."

"Like I said, good for you then."

"I think you might know the man who did it, too."

"I would?" Carter wished he had that coffee to give his hands something to do.

"He owns that Mexican place, Mesa Grande. You been there, right?"

"I thought a woman owned it."

"She does now, I suppose."

Carter waited out the silences. He had nothing but time.

"It was her husband."

"Sorry to hear that. I do like that place. Go there a lot."

"Yeah. Saw your truck there again on the traffic cameras."

"Big Brother always watching us, huh?"

"Not like in the city."

"Feels like it, the way you keep bringing it up."

DeFore rubbed his hands together. "Y'know what? Maybe I will take a Coke if you got one."

Carter stood and went to the fridge. He took his time, and with his back to DeFore, he let out a long breath, steadying himself. He got two bottles and set them on the table. He put his against the side of the table, the edge just under the cap, and then slapped down on the top of his bottle. The cap popped off, and he moved the neck quickly into his mouth to catch the foam bubbling from the top.

After he swallowed, he said, "My wife would never let me do that. But go ahead."

There was a small scar on the side of the table from where Carter had opened other bottles. DeFore followed suit, and soon, both of them were fighting belches.

"That all you wanted to tell me?" Carter said.

"I guess so. Been a strange time in town. This sort of thing isn't common for us at all."

"Thank God for that."

"Yeah. I guess if we're to look at the bright side, the only people who died this time were some real bad apples."

Carter smiled with the bottle almost to his lips. He pulled it back down again. "You can speak freely with me, detective. They were assholes."

DeFore smiled. "Yeah. Real assholes."

Carter raised his bottle in a bit of a toast, then drank. DeFore stood. He tilted his bottle back and swallowed the rest. He let out a belch and set the empty down.

"Thanks for the drink."

Carter nodded his acknowledgment.

DeFore took a small piece of paper from his pocket. He set it down on the kitchen table between them.

"What's this?" Carter asked.

"It's a name. And an address."

"Okay." Carter waited for him to explain.

"Lot of bad men out there, Mr. McCoy. A lot of them the law seems powerless to get. One reason or another, they slip through our fingers."

"That's too bad."

DeFore made a sour face. "So many rules and regulations. Tiny things that can get a case thrown out or set a man walking free, even when you know he did it."

"Did what?"

"Could be anything." He pointed to the paper absently, not a sharp arrow of a point, but making notice of it. "Rape, say. Multiple times. Statutory and otherwise."

"Another asshole."

DeFore nodded. "You could say that."

"Probably deserves the same thing those other boys got."

"Deserves to rot in hell, you mean. You're right. Should get a trial and a defense attorney. But last time, that lawyer got him off. So what he deserves and what the law provides are sometimes two different things."

"Ain't that the truth."

DeFore rapped his knuckles on the table twice, picking up the habit from his chief. "Well, I'll leave you be. I know you're busy."

"Me?" Carter laughed. "I got nothing but time."

"Okay. Well..." He nodded to the table, the paper there. "If you have the time."

DeFore walked out, and Carter heard the door open and shut. He didn't touch the paper. He replayed the conversation in his head. He wanted to be sure he understood it, didn't miss anything. He thought he knew what was being asked of him.

Chester stepped up next to him, laid his head on Carter's knee, and looked at him with tired eyes.

"They say you can't teach an old dog new tricks." He scratched at Chester's ears. "I think we both know that's not true."

Carter looked at the paper, but didn't pick it up. He didn't read the name or address. Not yet. There was time.

Acknowledgements

Thank you to Wayne Arthurson and the team at The Rights Factory. Thanks also to Shawn and the Level Best team and extended family of authors. Thanks to Laura McHugh, Joe Reid, David Swinson, Halley Sutton for the kind words. As always, to Marie, Molly and Gracie.

Photo by Mark Krajnak

About the Author

Eric Beetner is the author of more than 30 works of crime and thriller fiction. He's received an ITW award nomination, as well as nominations for a Shamus, a Derringer and three Anthony awards. Ken Bruen called him, "The new maestro of Noir." and LitReactor said he was "the 21st century's answer to Jim Thompson." He works as a TV editor and producer and has earned 7 Emmy nominations.

SOCIAL MEDIA HANDLES:
  Twitter/X – @ericbeetner
  IG – ericbeetner
  Facebook – Eric Beetner

AUTHOR WEBSITE:
  www.ericbeetner.com

Also by Eric Beetner

The Lars & Shaine trilogy:
The Devil Doesn't Want Me
When The Devil Comes To Call
The Devil At Your Door

The McGraw trilogy:
Rumrunners
Leadfoot
Sideswipe

The List series (with Frank Zafiro):
The Backlist
The Short List
The Getaway List

Standalones:
There and Back
All The Way Down
Two In The Head
Criminal Economics
The Year I Died Seven Times
Dig Two Graves
Dark Duet (White Hot Pistol & Blood On Their Hands)
Nine Toes In The Grave
Stripper Pole At The End Of The World
Over Their Heads (with JB Kohl)
A Bouquet of Bullets (stories)
The Sound Of Breaking Bones (A Grifter's Song series)
Burritos & Bullets (Guns and Tacos series)
Split Decision (Fight Card series)

A Mouth Full Of Blood (Fight Card series)

The Ray & Fokoli series:
  One Too Many Blows To The Head
  Borrowed Trouble